Tales of Bogles and Brownies – Kennedy Smith

Best wishes

Kennedy Smith

60 Anson Ave

Falkirk

FK1 5JE

TALES OF BOGLES & BROWNIES

Kennedy Smith

• KANDA PUBLICATIONS •

Published in 2022 by Kanda Publications

Publishing services provided by Lumphanan Press
www.lumphananpress.co.uk

Cover design by Fiona Campbell & Jim Hay

Printed & bound by Imprint Digital, UK.

ISBN: 978-0-9508238-2-9

I love a certain ladye;
So I wondered why my laughter grew
When first I saw her down by Yarm.
Perhaps it was that she laughed too
That banished shyness, made me calm.

This work is dedicated to my Ladye, Karty.

Contents

INTRODUCTION

... through the open doors
The harmless phantoms on their errands glide,
With feet that make no sound upon the floors.[1]

It happens to all of us at some time or other; there is some sort of happening we experience that we cannot explain by any logical process. Perhaps we dismiss it with, 'I must have been mistaken!' or some such expression and it is tucked away in the deep recesses of our history. If you take the trouble to recall and list such happenings, it starts you wondering if there is another world out there, another dimension, and just occasionally you accidently stray over that unmarked line. These tales, then, recount some such *strayings*.

In an earlier similar collection, *A Cantraip of Tales,* the stories ranged over a great variety of experiences most of them (marginally) mine. Here again, my history runs riot with reality. The title of this book hints that I delve into the worlds of ghosts and spirits; more than that, though, for they involve

1. From Haunted Houses – H. W. Longfellow

happenings that cannot be explained through our logic; it is above natural explanation; it is supernatural. Bishop Gavin Douglas in Eneados,[2] his sixteenth century translation of Virgil's Aeneas (into Scots) alerts the reader to the supernatural content of his work – *Of Brownyis and of Bogillis full is this Buke* – so too, I have alerted my readers by using the title: *Tales Of Bogles and Brownies.*

In these tales, I have frequently used my experiences from my various interests, be it music or prestidigitation, sailing or the wide-open spaces, industry or life. However, these are simply the bases from which I branch off into the realms of fantasy and the truth flies away in favour of effect. Treat the result as entertainment, not Gospel truth although, no doubt, some may strike a chord with your own experiences. Anyway, enjoy the experience of this collection of yarns, this stumble into the world *Of Bogles and Brownies.*

2. Eneados – Gavin Douglas 1513, printed 1553

MUSIC

THEY SAY THAT MUSIC IS as old as the hills – and who am I to question that! Even before man roamed the earth, there was sound, the progression of waves through a gaseous atmosphere. Out there in inter-stellar space where gaseous volumes are rare, there is no sound; how they must envy us.

Back in the days of the dinosaur, great beasties roared at one another, a music of sorts; I've even heard singers like that. Nevertheless, there were more gentle sounds like the sighing of the wind through the giant fern-like trees or the chuckling of waves on a shore – sounds that beguile us still. Why do you think people like to have trees in their gardens or choose to live by the sea? Plato once said (maybe more than once): *Music is a moral law. It gives soul to the universe, wings to the mind, flight to the imagination and charm and gaiety to life and to everything.* He said it in Greek, naturally.

As a hunter, early man would imitate bird song to help ensnare his dinner. Later as a planter, he would play on a flute to calm his herd, to protect his dinner. In more modern times, he would have background music to help the work along and thus to pay for his dinner. Do you remember the wartime scheme *Music While You Work?* Perhaps not! Music has always been there.

Nowadays, we are perhaps more sophisticated, more choosy about our music. It depends on our mood at that particular moment and indeed there are times when we just long for quiet. There are other times when the performer is more important to us than the music. If I am searching for a singer of love songs, I go for an oldie like Nat King Cole and a 1940s number. If I wish for Romantic music to wallow in, I lie with closed eyes on my chaise longue and listen to Rachmaninov's 2nd Symphony. For just pure beauty, I listen to the music which enchanted Mozart, the Miserere by Allegri. But the most pleasurable side of music, I find, is to play music and to play it with others, the social aspect. Not only is it pleasurable but also fulfilling. It doesn't really matter the proficiency of the performer; it's the excitement and fun of making music. You don't need an audience – indeed in my case, perhaps it's better without one.

It seems that music can be a reflection of your current emotion; it may even control your emotion, *to soothe the savage breast* to quote Congreve. There have even been times when I, a truly staid Scot, have felt my eyes well with tears through the beauty of an *adagio.* Of course, there have been other tears, tears of frustration during practice time.

Music is my business. To be more accurate, I play music as a profession in a symphony orchestra and the viola is my instrument. They say that it suits my temperament; perhaps it's because I am tall, my hair is jet black and is slicked straight back and with a widow's peak. You could say I am lugubrious, but I'm not really dismal. However, I am unpopular to sit behind because of my height. Those behind me complain that they can't see the conductor, which can be an advantage in some cases. I do have a special gift though, for I can hear Earth Music which carries my thoughts away to some other world and is often mistaken for moroseness.

When we talk about music, we often reflect the sounds produced by nature. Few of us can recognise the music of the earth. These are not the jarring sounds of an earthquake, but the sensations of sound or of music drifting up from the depths as we walk by or sit in contemplation. Have you ever noticed a tarmacked road on a hot day after a sudden sharp shower. Wraiths of steam rise and waft around in apparent haphazard motion. The music of the earth is like that. It rises in superficial to-ing and fro-ing, a languid motion that seems without reason or design. Its sensuous shimmy appears meaningless to the ill informed. Yet there is a pattern to all this randomness. Only a few of us recognise this. So – the next time you see me sitting with head tilted as in a dwam, you will know that I am listening to Earth Music.

By chance, I have noticed that this Earth Music varies depending on the location. Walking across a meadow with grazing cows, the sound wafting from the ground suggests to me that this has not always been a luscious green pasture but a place of trees casting leaves in season and providing shade for creatures of yore. The music then stretches back a few millennia, and I sense the movement of oceans below and creatures marine. Moving to the coolness of a pine forest and to its terpene scent, the Earth Music transforms to a nuance of tranquillity with sensuous movement synchronised with the swaying trees. It is almost as though the Earth Music takes on the character of its environment. And why not! I would have expected such empathy.

I don't know why I should have such rapport with Earth Music. I suppose it's akin to the water diviner with a dowsing stick, the difference being that the diviner is searching for something substantial that is there. Earth Music diffuses from the history of the place.

In general, I don't mind the gift, if you can call it that. There are times, though, when I can see it far enough. I don't feel comfortable in cemeteries and try to avoid such places. I feel I am eves dropping on the private thoughts of the inmates. I just do not wish to hear about the missed opportunities of someone's past even though they are expressed in such exquisite sounds. The anger of lost chances grates on the senses and lost love tears the soul apart.

There are occasions, too when I have to pass through the local cemetery, when perhaps I wish to attend a friend's funeral, all too often these days. It was on one such occasion that I became aware of a fragment of Earth Music with peculiar timbre which startled me somewhat. It jarred on the senses and sent shivers through my system. Listening carefully, the music suggested a sinister undercurrent which was disturbing. I could just make out a vague 'Help me,' and various other words which I couldn't decipher initially. I moved my position to clarify the tones and could just hear strains of 'Why did you kill me, Charlie?'

I took myself away from that spot and completed my visit as soon as decent; but the experience unnerved me for the rest of the day and for some time after. Who was the source of this cry from the grave, and more to the point, who was Charlie?

To say that I was distracted for some days after, is putting it mildly. It bothered me throughout the day, the evening and well into the night, dragging me down to such an extent that my playing was affected. I could get no solace from my viola or from the company of the orchestra. My friends noticed but I could tell them nothing; for really, I knew nothing. I had to return to the site to find out more.

Returning to the cemetery, I searched around to try and pick up the Earth Music and for a time, all that I could determine were the various complaints of the diverse residents, missed chances and the like. All day, I wandered around the wraiths of sound eddying about the mounds and headstones, mixing with apparitions of fret and fretting guests. The few individuals I encountered looked at me by dint of my strange behaviour, giving me a wide berth. I suppose I deserved their reaction, for my sombre appearance on such a miserable day would alarm the most mundane. Nowhere could I locate that cry for help.

I returned the next day and the day after that without success. Then on the fourth day, approaching dusk, I heard the call again; 'Help me!' There before me and almost obscured by some neighbouring vegetation, I located a headstone of black granite. I brushed away the surrounding growth and was able to make out the inscription on the stone's polished surface: "Jane Gordon Forbes," and the dates, "20th January 1982 – 21st June 2017," followed by "Beloved Wife of Charles Forbes." Below that was the after thought, "R.I.P." I scribbled a note of the epitaph and made sure of the location of the grave.

I debated what to do next. This must be the business of the police and I duly made my way to the local police station. It was a local branch and subsequently had not been updated recently, nor indeed ever. Entering the reception area, really battered from serious use, I rang a desk bell and waited before the sergeant on duty came from a back opening. I waited for him to say "Evenin' all," but instead it was, "Can I help?"

"I don't really know how to start. It's like this." I told him all about what I did for a living (name and job duly noted) and where I lived (again noted) and then tried to explain about Earth Music. By this time a constable colleague had joined the sergeant.

"I was walking through Glenfield Cemetery when I heard this cry for help coming from the grave of Jane Forbes;" then added lamely; "She died three years ago." The two policemen looked at one another and I could just imagine what thoughts were going through their minds.

When I had finished my sorry story, the sergeant looked me straight in the eye with, "Leave it with us, sir," and I think I could see a trace of a smirk from the constable. As I left the station that murky evening, I could guess the conversation between the two officers – *another nut case,* or *we get them every day* – or something similar. I'm not surprised really for I can hardly believe my own story.

My problem is that I can't leave anything unresolved. It's just not in my nature. I really am a nut case. Yet what could I do next? I had already decided to return the following day. Meantime, I worried away at the problem, tossing it this way and that and finding that I didn't know where my search was going. Another restless night!

Early next day, I returned to Glenfield Cemetery and made my way to the half hidden headstone. I stood there looking at the inscription for some time, searching for inspiration. Ceaselessly I paced to and fro and stop; to and fro and stop. What to do? Perhaps I could go to Charles Forbes' and confront him with his wife's message; or perhaps not. Anyway, I don't know his address. Perhaps I could find out where he lives.

Already a plan was forming in my addled brain. Looking behind the stone and brushing away the undergrowth, I could just make out the lair number. With this information, I approached the site office where such particulars are registered. "I wonder if I could please check the information about this lair? Is it for two or for four?" I asked. I must have appeared genuine in my dark suit and jet hair for in a moment the appropriate documents were produced together with the address of Charles Forbes. I duly noted down this information, all with no questions asked. "Thank you and goodbye."

I really wasn't sure what to do next. There was no point in going back to the police for I would get the same response as last time. I had no choice really but to face up to Mr Forbes and pass on the message from the grave, all quite innocently of course. I was playing in a concert that evening so I could call in on my way there. Yes, that's what I'll do; and the concert will be a good excuse for not lingering afterwards, if there is an afterwards. Of course on the other hand, if Charlie did kill Jane, maybe he wouldn't hesitate to add another to his tally – me.

Early evening and I prepared for the concert. Wearing black dinner suit and black shirt, as is the custom for orchestral concerts these days, I checked over my instrument and resined the bow. The instrument went into the boot of my car and I drove in the direction of the theatre muttering a desperate prayer. There ahead of me was a neat unimposing bungalow, the Forbes' residence and my interim destination.

Sitting there in my car before the garden gate, I took a few deep breaths; then hauled my gangling form from the vehicle. I stood staring at the house for a few long moments, then resolutely strode to the front door. I caught my reflection in the glass partition, dignified but perhaps funereal, and rang the bell. Through the glass, I could see a female form advancing to answer my call. She opened with a "Yes?"

"I wonder if I could speak with Mr Forbes, Mr Charles Forbes?"

She grunted and turned away. "Charlie! Someone for you."

A clatter and grumbling preceded Forbes' trek to the door. He was not what I expected. He was forty-five perhaps fifty years old with a highly florid complexion and a permanent scowl. Had I got the right person?

"Mr Forbes? Mr Charles Forbes? Husband of the late Jane Gordon Forbes?" I asked.

He startled back a shade and if anything his florid complexion became more florid. "What of it?" he demanded but with a degree of uncertainty.

The quicker I get this finished the better, I thought. "I received a cry for help from Jane. She wants to know why you killed her;" straight out, no gentle leading up to the point.

At this, he gave a gasp. "Who are you?" and his mouth hung open as he staggered back and onto a wooden kist. His face twisted and he leaned to one side as the lady of the house dived forward. Time for me to go! And as I left the house I could hear her phoning for the emergency services.

The concert that evening passed in a daze and that was the end of the affair; or so I thought. I just couldn't let the thing hang in the air like that. To a large extent I did just that but I did keep an eye on the local paper to see if there was any report of the incident – not a cheep! – until four days later, there it was in the obituary column; "Charles Forbes, 46 … suddenly … husband of second wife, Greta … funeral arrangements …" Nothing more; although I did hear a tale going round of a sighting; the presence of a strange figure, some say, was the Grim Reaper. I've been called worse things.

THE DEBT

I DROVE MY CAR ASHORE from the CalMac ferry and checked that my luggage was secure on the roof rack. It had been an uneventful trip from Mull through a kind sea, with the usual pod of dolphins bow-riding before they got bored and went off to charm some other boat. A basking shark sauntered past waving a languid dorsal fin. I waved back.

I had finished my job in Ayrshire as a chemist with a fertiliser factory and I just longed to blow the acid fumes from my lungs and breathe in the pure nectar of island air. I stood there next the open door of the car and drew in lung-fulls, the perfume of blossoms and, if I surmised correctly, a touch of *uisge-beatha.* I had taken up the post of assistant manager at the island whiskey distillery on the island of *Eilean-mara* and no doubt I would be the assay officer too as I was qualified as a Chartered Chemist.

"Good day to you!" I greeted the ancient mariner seated next a stack of lobster creels.

He nodded, "Aye," and returned to his day dreaming.

"Could you direct me to Bay House, please?"

He pondered briefly, "Och, that will be the big grey building up there, chust past the post office." He pointed vaguely up the sole road of the village and added, "You will be the new manager, then?"

"Assistant manager," I corrected and he smiled at some private secret.

I jumped in my car and drove up the hill as directed and spotted Bay House, very grey and rather bleak. I parked the car on its surrounding pebble driveway near the front door just as the rain started. The drizzle chased me through the unlocked front door and I shook the droplets from my tweed jacket.

"Oh, 'tis yourself. Come away in and warm yourself by the fire and I'll make a cup of tea," a hidden voice called. "You will be after feeling the cold, you being from the south. I'm Mrs Ferguson, here to look after the house for you while you are here." Enter Mrs Ferguson, a matronly lady, who then hustled away and I could hear the rattle of a kettle in the distant kitchen.

Looking round at my new home, it seemed warm enough in front of the welcoming fire but I could detect more than a hint of fusty dampness in the air. The furnishings suggested Victorian times and had probably come with the original house. The drapes were blue velvet sorely faded at the edges with matching threadbare dark blue carpets. It would do me well enough for now. I don't expect I would be staying here forever and I could make myself comfortable for now, no doubt.

Mrs Ferguson bustled in with a tray and laid out two cups with some jam scones. I eyed them longingly. "You will be after staying here until you can find somewhere of your own," she stated. "There are one or two cottages up for sale – och, but you will have time enough to go looking."

I nodded and munched. The sea voyage had sharpened my appetite. We continued talking about nothing much for a bit. She was a great talker, was Mrs Ferguson.

"You will have seen the brewing place on your way up," she continued. "It is that great white building over by the quay side. Callum – that will be the manager – runs the place with a few lads from the village. It is good that there is some local work for the men-folk."

So it went on till I rose from my armchair and went off to bring in my luggage. "Where can I put my stuff, Mrs Ferguson?" and she went off leading me to a first floor room. I dumped my stuff in the middle of the floor of a very large and very cold bedroom. I thought, 'The sooner I find a proper place the better'.

"I will be leaving you to get on with your unpacking while I get your dinner prepared;" and with that she hastened off rustling as she went. I wouldn't be surprised if her dress were Victorian too.

After my meal, I took a stroll round the village in spite of the drizzle. It was a neat little place complete, I noticed, with its own pub. (Mental note.) There didn't seem to be any 'for sale' notices on any of the cottages; perhaps they were a bit coy about things like that. The focus of the village was, of course, the whiskey distillery, all gloriously white. It was a Saturday so I didn't venture inside. It would have been pointless anyway, for the offices would be empty although there would be a weekend workforce about. All appeared tidy and ship-shape, as any efficient outfit should be.

My wandering took me down to the quay with its flotilla of small boats sheltering there. I expect I would have my own vessel too were I to stay here for any length of time. Many of the craft were working boats, essentially for lobster fishing, for there were many creels around in little discrete clumps. The bouquet of the sea assailed the senses mingled with the reek of fish past their prime – all the pleasures of a small port. The heavy duty quay for the ferry was a separate structure and had been exorcised to a site further north.

The next day was dry. Perhaps this would give me an opportunity to explore the village and meet some of the locals; and where better to meet them than the pub. After a cereal breakfast and lukewarm coffee, I made my way down the hill towards the harbour. The village seemed deserted and to make things worse, the pub was closed. Where is everyone? Of course, this is the Highlands; this is the Sabbath. Nothing happens on the Sabbath, not even a decent breakfast. I just had to content myself with a lone stroll through a bleak village.

I made it to the top end of the group of houses where the road gave way to a rough track. I carried on to the brow of the hill and looked back at the sprawl of houses and beyond. The sea extended to a band of blue on the horizon, one of the neighbouring islands. The peace of the place was palpable, not a breath of wind with only the occasional call of a lone whaup to break the silence. I was beginning to feel apprehensive and wondered about the wisdom of my taking a post in this remote place.

Returning to the grey house I could feel the village stirring. I met various folk on their way to church and acknowledged the curt greetings. They obviously had me marked down as a heathen. Soon, strains of a psalm drifted from the wee white kirk, first the cantor followed by the congregation. It was a strange unearthly sound which seemed to penetrate my whole being. It was the Kirk's version of plain chant though they would probably double mark me as a heathen for saying so. The ululating sound haunted me for the rest of the stroll.

There was no sign of Mrs Ferguson when I returned, but there was a cold collation of various meats, some bread and cold semolina pudding with a dash of anonymous red jam plonked on its summit. Anyway, I like semolina pudding, preferably with lumps. I was learning quickly about the Sabbath.

I spent the rest of the day exploring the rest of the rambling house and promptly decided that I must find somewhere smaller and cosier. I could look after myself. I could cook. I could tidy. I could wash floors or whatever else was required – I think.

The next day, the Monday, I arrived at the distillery early and into the main office. Looking round, the atmosphere of tidiness was evident. There seemed to be a typists' room with two places. Two further offices led me to the conclusion that this was almost a cottage industry, nevertheless with big bucks at the end of the day.

At this point Mr McKenzie breezed in with a bright "Good Morning". I had already met him at my interview in Glasgow. We exchanged further pleasantries before we were interrupted by Jenny, his secretary (THE secretary) with tea to brighten up the morning.

Down to business. He (call me Callum) explained the process from the malting loft, through mashing, fermentation to distillation. Then the important part, the maturation in 'second hand' wooden barrels. I say 'second hand' and I suppose they were; for the barrels had either been previously used to mature bourbon whiskey or (for special customers) sherry barrels. He followed up his lecture with a tour around the working plant, finishing in maturation. That is where the whiskey is kept to mature in barrels.

The barrels seemed to be unusual in that they had some sort of coating, a translucent skin. I kneeled down to look closer.

"Oh, that's some daft idea of Head Office. They reckon that we are losing too much product through evaporation from the barrels; so we've had to spray the barrels with this plastic coating;" and Callum sniffed in disapproval.

"Surely it affects the taste," I observed. "It needs air to help it mature."

Callum nodded in despair. "That's what I told them, but they insisted. They got the idea from some high-flying scientist Johnie – who knows nothing of brewing. He just insists that he is always right." Callum moved on shaking his head.

We moved back to the office. He continued moaning and muttering to himself until Jenny brought more tea. It looked like this was the normal drill for such bouts.

I soon fell into the ways of the distillery. The tea (regularly), strolls around the process to check the operation, the collection of samples and their analyses, all routine. Time passed pleasantly enough and the village itself was agreeable. It had a therapy all its own.

After a short settling in, Callum remarked, "You'll have to come down to The Vik this evening and have a dram," and seeing my puzzled reaction, "the pub, The Viking Pub. There'll be live music and I can introduce you to some of the locals."

That evening, I did just that and in the midst of the fiddle music and the general fug, I was introduced to many of the local worthies – and promptly forgot their names. It was a pleasant evening. I enjoyed their friendly company and interesting tales. More to the point, I found out that there was a cottage for sale at the top end of the village.

It was a snug enough cottage and would suit me fine. I suppose it was a bit remote being further uphill yet I expect the daily walk would do wonders for my figure – long overdue. I moved my few belongings in before the end of spring and bade Mrs Ferguson farewell. I had the feeling that she was glad to see the back of me. Bay House reverted to its former use as accommodation for business visitors to the distillery.

Spring drifted into summer and summer into autumn. Life was pleasant enough and I even managed to find myself a small boat for occasional fishing for the evening meal. However, I only managed to catch the occasional mackerel and I soon grew tired of their oily taste. The mild days were often veiled in soft rain, not that I noticed within the confines of the distillery. I did notice that Callum was uneasy and spent much of his day gazing into the distance. I had the feeling that he was troubled about the plastic covered barrels and what it was doing to his beloved whiskey. Samples from the barrels seemed to be overloaded with fusel oil and in particular amyl alcohol.

My occasional visits to The Vik were always welcomed for I had an extensive repertoire of bar tricks and I was always pleased to try them out on someone new. A bonus, too, were the frequent drams and my glass was regularly kept topped up. Many were the autumn evenings when I would trace an uncertain path to my sanctuary, my white cottage by the hill.

On one such evening, the wind had risen and I guessed we were in for a bit of a blow. My coat flapped around my legs causing me to stagger and in the dusk I imagined all sorts of spectres and bodachs sheltering beyond every hawthorn thicket or in the darker leeway of a cottage. I staggered, left and right, oblivious to any traffic; but of course, there was no traffic. Nor was there any street lighting. The council didn't stretch to such luxuries. Who or what were these shades?

The following day was a working day and my head was thick with hangover. I thought the walk to work would clear things, but no such luck. I arrived in the office, no doubt grumpy and glaring at everyone. For once, Jenny brought me coffee rather than tea. She recognised the signs. Callum was too preoccupied to notice that anything was amiss. He didn't say anything, merely sat at his desk staring into space. Later, I went off to the laboratory to complete the analysis on a sample from a barrel. The remainder I took back to the office to cheer up the boss. He took a sip from the beaker and let it rest on his tongue before spitting it out.

"Eugh! That's terrible. Is that the best we can produce?" He twisted his face in disgust. "That's what I mean. All this plastic coating is ruining the maturation."

I could only agree with him though I didn't have his sensitive palate.

Autumn blew in winter with a force 9 westerly. Luckily, or by design, the village was in the lea of *Eilean-mara* and was largely sheltered by hills. Nevertheless, I could feel my little cottage shake under the battering. It was typical of Hebridean winters; black stormy days and even blacker nights.

The storm eased a bit after three days and I decided to celebrate by a visit to The Vik – any excuse. I had a new trick in my pocket, one with a matchbox. A couple of card tricks and an hour later, I judged that it was time to hit the road and I duly donned my coat and bade the rest *oidhche mhath leat,* good night.

It was still angry in the turbulent black of the night and gusts tossed me from one side of the road to the other. I steeled myself against the wind battering my face and at times, the tempest forced me back on my heels. Never did my walk to the cottage seem so long. All was full of undercurrents, with threats of unknown perils and the menace of bogles and wraiths of the dead.

The wind through the wires overhead sang the songs of banshees, ululating in their own close harmonies, rivals to the Kirk psalms. All this attacked my ears on that lone walk. And all this time there seemed to be a flapping mingled in the noise of the storm, not of my coat as previously but some new dimension of sound. I shivered.

For some reason, I looked round as you do on such a night. There was a faint glimmer radiating from the sea in the bay and there, silhouetted was a giant M-shape with rippling edges the likes of which I had never before experienced. An object in the middle of the M turned to reveal a face so grotesquely beyond description. An utterance, I cannot call a voice, said, "I've come - to collect - the debt."

Without an answer from a petrified me, it continued, "I

have come for the Angels' Share." And the echoes of "Angels' Share" ranged round and round in my head.

That night in my cottage, I finished off an entire half bottle of malt.

They say that when I arrived for work next day, I kept repeating over and over, "Angels' Share … Angels' Share …" and they started stripping the plastic sheaths from the barrels.

TAXI

It had been difficult for me recently, difficult at work, difficult at home. I suppose the setbacks at work had affected my moods at home and there was no doubt about it, that my health was being affected. These breathless spells and palpitations were happening with increased frequency, so really this convention had come at an opportune time. It would give me a bit of a rest and a change of environment.

As a variation from their usual, the firm had booked me into a really posh room complete with *en suite.* There were the usual basic furniture items, a pleasant view over rolling fields and, of all things, a small drinks cabinet complete with miniature fridge. Leaving my luggage in the middle of the room, I collapsed onto the bed for forty winks before joining the others down in the conference hall.

In that brief period, my mind went over the events of recent weeks. I had worked hard trying to get the last three booklets edited and into a presentable form to send out to our main customer. I did not fancy yet another journey to Ruabon in Wales to discuss some minor detail in the text that they wanted amended. I took the stuff home and spent most evenings dictating changes to a machine. Everything round me seemed to be a machine, to be talked to or cursed at and I think my good lady was getting really tired of my behaviour. I really must take myself in hand, spend more time with her, calm myself down. Strange visions passed through my mind, peculiar shapes and colours. In one corner of my mind, there was a rainbow, not a normal rainbow, for the colours were all muddy. The streak of yellow caught my attention generating paroxysms of tension and anxiety. On reflexion, it was probably the accumulation of all the work of the past several weeks catching up.

I woke abruptly and gazed around at the unfamiliar surroundings. Of course, that's it. I'm at this conference on publishing. I must go down to the foyer and find out the programme for the afternoon. With a bit of luck, I should be able to snooze, unobtrusively of course, through most of the proceedings. Rather a grand staircase led me down to the main reception area. I stood there in the hotel foyer gazing around me with question mark eyes when one of the assistants approached me. 'Your taxi has arrived, sir' and he pointed to the door. I obediently stepped out to the marble steps and nodded at the doorman. Yes! There it was, the taxi with its uniformed driver in peaked cap. I opened the door and tumbled into the back and duly belted up.

'Where to?' the driver asked. But my mind was blank. I didn't know where I was going or indeed why.

The driver glanced in his driving mirror, no doubt saw the puzzled expression and nodded. 'The usual place then?' I could only give an approving nod and off we set.

Intent on finding out more, I set about trying to strike up some sort of conversation with my driver. 'Been in this job long?' I asked.

'Oh, it seems like forever.'

That didn't get me far. 'This is a nice comfortable vehicle you have here.'

'We try to please.'

So much for that! 'I'm not familiar with this make.'

That resulted in a non-descript 'Mmm'.

'Had it for long, then?'

'Oh quite a while! I had a coach and pair before this and I've even had to share a sedan chair.'

It sounded like he was taking the Michael and I fell silent for a bit. Various buildings flashed by, none of them familiar although I thought I recognised St. Mark's Church; but I couldn't be sure. At first it seemed we were driving through a tunnel of stone, merging now into red brick followed by some ramshackle wooden structures. Next I would expect wattle and mud, I thought sardonically.

The light outside was fading somewhat, a bit early in the evening for this time of year. I glanced at my watch and to my surprise, it wasn't on my wrist. I must have left it back at the hotel. I didn't remember taking it off. A sort of mist-come-fog was starting to form outside and I guessed that accounted for the poor light.

'Do you think this fog will delay us?' I asked.

'Nothing delays us. We are always on time no matter the conditions. The Paradise Club is just ahead.'

'The Paradise Club? I don't think I've been there before.'

'No, I don't expect you have,' the diver exclaimed; and he actually smiled, albeit an enigmatic smile.

By this time, buildings had been left behind and we seemed to be travelling though some countrified region, mostly trees and some scrubby undergrowth.

'Almost there now,' he said as we swept through a bolt of trees and forded a shallow stream with a partly obscured notice just showing 'ST … ' I expect it was 'Saint something.' There before us was a magnificent house, all lit up, almost expecting us. The driver stopped under a stone archway, evidently the building's entrance and a flunky stepped forward to open the door of the taxi. No sooner had I paid my two pence fare (two pence?) when the vehicle sped off into the dusk. All alone I looked around but could discern nothing familiar. There was the subdued hubbub of many, perhaps celebrating - what, I couldn't say. I turned to enter the Paradise Club.

The main door opened into an extensive reception area milling with folks of all sorts, dressed in all their finery. Desperately I looked around for a recognisable face and over on the far side, there was Kenneth. I pushed my way through the throng and greeted him warmly, pleased really to see something familiar. 'Hi, Ken, long time no see! I thought you were dead.'

He turned and smiled. 'I am.'

AN T-EILEAN

I HAVE TWO PASSIONS IN life, music and boats. The former is my job (or rather, was my job), for now I have had to quit my post in the NYP for health reasons; I have a trapped nerve in my left shoulder which precludes me playing for long periods and certainly from symphonic concerts. As for boats, my age limits my physical activity to short cruises.

Here I am then on this 70ft boat, the Morning Star. It was formerly a rescue vessel with the Norwegian fishing fleet and we are leaving Oban to tour the Scottish Western Isles. Not to be completely divorced from music, I have brought a violin with me. I have done this before and occasionally park myself on the sundeck and play some Scottish airs. It all adds to the atmosphere.

Anyway, we set out on a pleasant enough Saturday evening – destination Tobermory. Soon after passing the South Lismore Light, the ship was in the Sound of Mull and over to our right – or should that be *starboard* (must get used to these nautical terms) – a radiant rainbow bent backwards over *Morvern* and just as quickly vanished before I could unpacked my camera. To port, the great bulk of Ben More shyly dodged behind its lesser neighbours, *Corra-bheinn* and *Sgurr Dearg* as we pressed on. Little boats and big ships danced past to the sound of the Kelpies whistling through the rigging and in the gathering dusk, *Tobermory* with its multi-coloured shirts appeared in the distance. That evening, we dined well, swinging gently on a mooring buoy in the bay.

Making our way westerly, there was *Muck* Island and *Eigg* too with its characteristic plook *(Allt a' Bhlair Dhuibh*) and soon the looming heights of Rum drew us onward to *Canna*. With the motion of the boat, the strains of the *Mingulay* Boat Song ran through my head … Heel y'ho boys / let her go boys / Bring her head round / into the weather … Soon we were in the lee of *Canna* and the rest of the trip was easier.

From the anchorage of *Canna*, we passengers set off in various directions to explore, some towards the island of *Sanday*, others to Compass Hill looking for golden eagles (unsuccessfully). I took the path to the castle-prison by way of a sandy shore and listened to *the little waves sliding up the shore and back, lisping all the way* (to quote MacCaig.) From the shore, I spotted a goldy soaring high and I'm sure it was sticking its tongue out at those on the hill. As a group, we met up again at the local café and had ice cream; what else!

Motoring down the lee of Mull the next day, there on its eastern shore in one of the many sandy inlets I spotted around a score of deer. Miffed, they turned to stare at us and gave us the V-sign with their ears.

The voyage south continued through green seas topped with heads of white spume. Over to the left (that should be port) barely visible were the Black *Cullens* with peaks hidden in low cloud. Occasionally, just occasionally, a shaft of sunlight would burst through and spill down the slopes before returning to the murk. On the right, the isle of *Muck* dodged behind its brawny neighbour, *Eigg*. We would not be stopping off at either island that day in view of the impending weather. A force 9 was forecast; that's a strong gale. We neared the *Skye* coast and my attention was drawn to some islands there. "What islands are those, Skipper?"

"That's the Island of *Soay*," he answered; "not THE *Soay* famous for its sheep. That one is in the *St. Kilda* group."

"What about the small island?"

The skipper shook his head and referred to the chart. "According to this, that is *Eilean a'dol à Sealladh* . It's a new one on me."

I looked at the little island for some time, its lush green topped with heather, its rugged shoreline with sand patches and a cave or two. Further round, I could see the ruins of a bothy.

Some impulse took me to the sun-deck with my fiddle and there in the gathering gloom, I serenaded the dolphins. Notes blew off in random tracks and byways across the white wave tops. It was only then that I noticed a strange corona lipping the edges of the Black *Cullens* of *Skye.* In particular, the little island seemed to glow in its own halo. I had never seen such a strange display. Perhaps it was a form of St. Elmo's Fire; I doubt if it was due to my playing but it did make me uneasy and I got off that so-called sun-deck mighty quickly. *Eilean a'dol à Sealladh* disturbed me, yet in some way drew me to its shores and strange thoughts plagued me for the rest of the evening.

Just west of Loch *Hourn* lies the tiny island of *Ornsay*

providing a favourite natural harbour. There, we planned to spend a sheltered night. In the event, it proved to be boisterous with the skipper periodically checking the anchor. Morning Star did rock but gently as Valkyries rode overhead and the Blue Men did their best below. You could almost hear Wagner smacking his lips.

Over breakfast, I tackled the skipper over a plan I had for that day. "I wonder if I could make a special request," I asked? He just looked at me without commenting. "I'm fascinated by that little isle we passed yesterday, *Eilean a'dol à Sealladh.*

"Oh yes," he declared uneasily. I could sense that he too felt the isle's oddness.

"Instead of going to *Eigg* as planned, you could drop me off at that little island for the day and collect me again in the evening on your way back to Loch *Hourn*."

After some little hesitation, "I'll get cook to make you up some sandwiches and we can arrange that," he replied with some disquiet.

So it was that I stepped ashore on *Eilean a'dol à Sealladh* and arranged to meet the boat at six on its return trip, with a hawthorn bush near the shore as a marker. I had my haversack with waterproofs, sandwiches, drink and mobile phone. Over my shoulder I slung the strap of my violin case, the instrument safely inside. It was good to be on my own and able to plan my day.

It was one of those days when it couldn't decide whether to rain or shine. I didn't wish to expose my fiddle to the elements so I retired to a cave and lifted the instrument from its case. I started with a gentle air, *Thro' the Wood, Laddie* and marvelled at the acoustics of the place. Then something a bit livelier with *The Soldier's Joy* and kindred dance tunes. How I enjoyed the delight of playing to the void, to the utter desolation.

Presently, I lay back, ate my sandwiches and drank the bottled water – *Quaff the nectar – cull the roses / Gather fruit and flowers in plenty!*[3] and after a time I fell into a doze.

I seem to have closed my eyes for a mere instant when I felt a persistent nudging. There before me was the strangest creature I have ever seen. Could it be an old man or some other ancient? Yet in spite of the spindle limbs, he seemed muscular and almost menacing. I edged away from The Being as he bent down and peered closely.

"*Seinn fidheall,*" he screeched. *"Seinn! Seinn fidhlear!"*

Seeing my blank, indeed terrified, look, he tried again. "Play your fiddle, fiddler! We are for having a *ceilidh* and you are the fiddler."

By now I could make out similar figures in the dark recesses of the cave and thought it best to fall in with his request, nae, command. Out came my violin and I tuned up. What should I play? I'll try *Thro' the Wood Laddie* again just to warm up and the strange creatures sat around in a circle listening.

When I had finished, their spokes-creature demanded, "Play some dances! We want to dance," and there was a murmur of agreement from the others.

So started the most unusual *ceilidh* of my life. I started with a reel, *The wind that Shakes the Barley* and it was the oddest reel I have ever seen. They moved round in one large circle

3. Gilbert and Sullivan from their opera, Utopia Ltd

going through a series of pirouettes and ending each phrase with a great stomping of feet. As the dance progressed, the rhythm increased and legs and arms flew everywhere in gay abandon. I had the feeling it was all made up spontaneously, for each individual had his own version. Peels of laughter and delight filled the cavern and as I finished the progression of numbers, one of the group brought me a drink in a porcelain cup murmuring "*Meadh.*" I tried the liquid and found it sweet with a slight odour of heather but strangely refreshing.

More playing, more dancing, more mead; so the time passed and all became more raucous and animated with legs kicking everywhere. There were strange boots and other bizarre footwear flying through the air. Ear splitting shouts and whoops echoed from the walls of the cave, through the reels and jigs in great shrieks of joy. And there I was, the centre of it all with my bow and fiddle. It had to end so I played a great lush chord and stopped the session.

I sipped the mead and amid cries of "*Aon uair eile*" and "more, more" I decided to play a slow Strathspey to calm things down. Not a bit of it! It was a Strathspey danced as I'd never seen it danced before. Instead of the stately progression with a little hop on the Scotch snap, it became a series of double pirouettes with a great leap on the snap, all athletic enough to be an Olympic event. The problem was that they all tried to outleap each other resulting in many mid-air collisions and bad tempered confrontations. I returned to the safer reels and jigs.

Time slipped by and the mead flowed. Before I knew it, I had drifted into a slumber. Voices faded and a cloud descended on my world.

The encroaching cold and a hangover wakened me. A quick glance at my watch told me it was nearly time for my lift back to this world; yet when I reached the tree there was nothing, no vessel, just an empty spread of sea. I waited and I could see that the light was fading. The hawthorn provided me with no shelter with its open lattice of elbows and oxters and the odd strand of bladder wrack. I could feel the chill of the evening as I tried to give them a call on my mobile only to discover that the battery was flat.

Darkness covered all as I stumbled back to the cave. No mead to heat me or company to greet me, be it real or a mere figment. I wore my waterproofs and huddled in a corner in an attempt to keep warm; but there was to be no merrymaking that night. My fiddle remained in its case.

It was a very stiff fiddler who emerged from the cave next morning. A wash and a drink from a nearby stream revived me somewhat, but I was in a foul mood. What had happened to the cruise ship? Had they deliberately left me to freeze? There would be many questions to answer when I catch up with them. Sitting under the hawthorn in my yellow waterproofs, I fumed.

After some time, a small fishing boat appeared lifting creels and after some frantic waving I managed to attract his attention. As he edged inshore, I waded out to meet him oblivious of the water filling my boots.

"Can you give me a lift to the mainland? I'll pay you well."

The lone fisherman seemed bemused and gestured me aboard. He appeared to be much older than I expected and reminded me of Hemmingway's 'The Old Man and the Sea.' His bare sinuous arms assisted me over the bulwark and dumped me like one of his lobster creels in the bilge water. "Och, no bother at all. I will be going to *Mallaig* anyway;" he answered in his Highland brogue and he pointed the craft eastwards.

Presently he asked; "And how would you be after getting marooned like that, all by yourself on a desert island? It's not the sort of place to be by yourself for long."

He turned to eye me and I could see the question marks; so I felt compelled to explain the circumstances. "I requested the skipper of the Morning Star to land me there and arranged for him to pick me up later. He just hasn't returned."

"The Morning Star, you say? Och, she's in Mallaig right now, or she was this morning. He will be pleased to see you, right enough."

I just sat there fuming, nursing my anger and my wet feet.

After a time, he asked, "Did you enjoy your visit to the wee island." I got the feeling that he was ribbing me for there was the hint of a twinkle there.

"Well enough," I grunted and let it go at that.

"It is a strange wee place to be visiting though I have not been on it myself, at all," he continued. "You will be after having a bit of a holiday, then?"

I grunted again but did not feel much like chatting to the man.

"You will be a fiddler then?" he persisted. Do you know Sawney Hamilton? He is weel kent in these parts. He is after playing at the ceilidhs and the like from here to Lochaber." His casual chatter went on and on about various fiddlers he had known and the famous Neil Gows of past times.

In what seemed like an eternity, the green navigation

light came into view and we sailed into the inner harbour. He brushed away my offer of payment and my warm thanks and motored back out to sea.

With my haversack and violin, I made my way along the key to the outer harbour. There, I clambered over two trawlers to reach The Morning Star where I dumped my haversack with a loud bump. Stamping my feet, I made for the bridge and the skipper's quarters. The door opened and he stood there. His face drained of all colour and turned a shade of paste. He staggered back and abruptly sat on his chart table. "You … you," he stammered, "It can't be. We looked everywhere," and was promptly sick.

This was not the reaction I expected.

We both withdrew to the stateroom and had large whiskeys. He eyed me up and down as though he was looking at some sort of vision or ghost. At last he managed to speak. "We looked everywhere. The island just seemed to have disappeared. What happened to you?"

"Me?" I shouted. "I waited all evening and you didn't turn up. There I was sitting under that damned bush and nothing. Nothing."

He looked bewildered. "There was no island," he said, "just no island." He seemed as baffled by the whole affair as I was. "This was so long ago. It must be around a year, yes, almost exactly a year."

I sat back, my head spinning as I tried to take this in. "I've been away for a year? It can't be!"

The skipper could see my confusion. "Where have you been and how did you get here," he asked?

"I cadged a lift from a fisherman who was lifting creels along that coast. He came into *Mallaig*, left me here and just made off."

"There are no lobsters in that area. He must have been after some other catch, I can't think what," the skipper exclaimed.

Then it struck me. The fisherman must have been one of the creatures delegated to see me safely home. "What does the island name mean - *Eilean a'dol à Sealladh."* I asked.

"Hey, Hamish," he shouted to one of the crew of the neighbouring fishing boat. "He's a Gaelic speaker. What is the meaning of *Eilean a'dol à Sealladh*, Hamish?"

There was a pause. "That would be, The Island that Vanishes."

PHOËBE

HAVING LIVED FOR SO MANY days, I sometimes look back and decide what are highlights and what are best forgotten. There are so many that fall into both categories that my mind is in turmoil and I am reluctant to look too closely at the past. However, there is one period which sticks out; for it has stayed with me; it has haunted me; and that is the love affair with Phoëbe.

I was living in Stockton-on-Tees at the time and I travelled by bus taking me past all sorts of businesses. It was on one of those occasions I spotted Phoëbe. I fancy it was love at first sight and there and then I resolved to go and see her at the weekend. This duly arrived and I stood there in the outskirts of Norton gazing at her. The asking price for this 1939 Jaguar open tourer was £75 which I didn't have at that precise moment. So! I just stood and looked.

Entering the makeshift premises, I had a good look at my sweetheart, the tyres, the bodywork in general and the interior. Phoëbe had certainly been around. A salesman is approaching. Now for the usual sales spiel pointing out her merits which seemed to amount to twin-tone horns and additional spotlights.

I was blind to her long list of faults, common in love at first sight. "Sit in and we'll have a spin around," he invited. I duly sat in and he closed my door, all very polite.

The engine fired first time and we roared out and onto the open highway. The salesman introduced himself as "Dixon; folks call me Bronco Dixon." I later found out that he had earned the name in his dirt track racing days. Driving back into the covered area, he caught part of the running board (yes, it had running boards; *v.* the gangster movies of the 1930s.) The result? He knocked off a couple of quid from the asking price.

Later, I raised the cash and off we roared.

I had a piece of waste ground near where I lived and on the middle thereof was my beloved Phoëbe. Her long bonnet of silver stretched forth in elegance not seen in today's models, set off against black wings that some call mudguards. Her knock-off wire wheels impatiently await the next expedition and her open top hides the rather battered drop head best kept anonymous – a replacement job for the near future. The chromed radiator over the vertical grill sported two headlights on stalks and two spotlights over the twin-toned horns. To crown all, above the radiator there was a naked lady in chrom. True, the lady showed signs of a former illness, judging by the array of pockmarks. Still, she was mine and I love her yet.

Now let us look at the working parts. I raised her bonnet and surveyed the engine. One and a half litres of power was hardly enough for such a large and heavy chassis. (I hope she didn't hear me.) Yet, it will have to do for the moment and she seemed to cope smoothly for her age. The electrics all seemed to operate though the large headlights swivelled at all angles when the mood took her, sometimes cross-eyed, other times huffy-eyed. The spots were OK though. The direction indicators were little flags that stuck out and lighted up when used. As for the twin tone horns, they gave the impression of a limousine, which she was in my eyes. I would have to be alert to the state of the battery with all these demands. As for her silencer, that gave up long ago and she roared like an aristocrat.

Phoëbe was a bit fussy and indeed finicky at times. For a start, she didn't like to get her feet wet. I found this out one singularly wet day when we had to run through some deep puddle. She refused to stop while I had to negotiate a tricky obstacle course. This was brought home when she again showed a reluctance to stop going down a steep hill. An overhaul of the brakes came to the top of the jobs-to-do list, a list that turned out to be long, long, long.

Beware the pretty face! All was not as it seemed and I had a feeling that there were many secrets lurking, just waiting for the moment, whether it be appropriate or not. I wont say that Phoëbe was temperamental but she certainly had a mind of her own – and stubborn with it. Indeed, there were times when she was downright awkward and other times when she was impetuous.

There was the occasion when we were overtaking a lorry and ping, we went off at full throttle. A quick switch off and we coasted into the nearest layby midst much banging from unburned petrol as she threw a tantrum. The spring controlling the accelerator had broken.

Then there was the time when giving my boss a lift to a site at another location. The engine started clattering, there was a dire smell of hot oil and the journey ended there and then. I think she was jealous and wished to embarrass me. In the event, it transpired that a broken oil line was to blame. Even so, it had me thinking. What untold matters lie in wait!

There was one event that did rebound somewhat. The passenger door had become badly hung over the years and sagged, catching the running board. Any time I had a passenger, I had to open their door from the outside lifting it over this obstruction. Thus, I gained a reputation for being such a polite young man. One up to me, Phoëbe!

Thus, over time there developed this love – hate relationship.

This is the trouble with these ladies; they are so baffling. One minute they are right as rain (except when they enter deep puddles); the next, they are a nightmare of contradictions; and always midst all, there forever seems to be an element of jealousy. Take that time I took Karty up to Kilmarnock to meet my parents. On the way back South, I had three punctures. The first was no problem for I had my spare. The second happened near the Solway area; now that *was* a problem, essentially because I had no puncture outfit or air pump. Ironically, I did have tyre levers. Dusk was falling and I thought I must seek some sort of help. As it happened, there was a lit-up dwelling nearby. That was my saviour with patch and foot-pump. The third puncture was more of a problem. It was pitch dark by then and we were just approaching Bowes/Brough moor, as lonely a place as any. All sorts of ideas were going through my mind when a policeman on bicycle approached. He had a bicycle puncture outfit which we used, but no suitable pump. His solution was to stop the first car that came along and to borrow their pump. Thus, we completed this misery in 12 hours; it should have taken 5 hours. I should say in explanation that tyres in those days had an inner tube; and everyone had a pump, except me. Ah jealousy!

Then there was the incident of the boulder; in truth it seemed like a boulder at the time. Again it was night time; again I was travelling from Kilmarnock to Teesside; again it was when crossing the bleak Bowes/Brough moor. This desolate stretch of heathland road has no proper edge and I happened to be travelling only on side lights to conserve the battery when there was an almighty bang. I had hit a roadside boulder or milestone or outcrop of some sort. I stopped to examine the damage. I had hit something very hard with the left hub.

Lets look at the damage, I thought and by the light of my torch I could see the marks on the knock-off hubcap – nothing more although the nearside headlight seemed loose. That was all – until I started moving again. It was evident that the front wheels were out of alignment judging by the sound of squealing tyres. Thus Phoëbe sobbed and squealed all the way home. It struck me, though, when driving through Darlington that we sounded like Chicago gangsters making their getaway after a raid. We made it - No cops!

All these 'incidents' had me thinking; perhaps I had misjudged Phoëbe. Here was I thinking that these mishaps were the result of jealousy or spite on her part, but conceivably, was there some quite different motive? Looking at the various episodes, the two big dramas were during journeys back to Teesside. Maybe she didn't like the area, or the atmosphere there. Yes! That's it. Between the chemical pollution and the salt-laden air, the area was ripe for corrosion and Phoëbe had seen plenty of that over the years.

I'll test my theories, I thought. I'll take a trip to Saltburn, a local seaside town and see how she reacts to all that salt air. I had sorted out the problems with the headlight and the wheel alignment and off we sped towards the salty coast.

We didn't get there and ever since I've blamed myself for what happened. There was a bang from the rear and the engine stopped driving, not the engine's fault for it was roaring away. It was just that the wheels stopped turning. A broken half-shaft, I thought – and it was. Just to be sure, I started to jack-up the car. The jack rose but the car did not – and the jack rose further as the chassis bent in protest. Phoëbe just gave up at that point and abandoned this life. She was gone forever.

BIRDS OF A DIFFERENT FEATHER

My first brush with education was at the local village school. I enjoyed my time there yet I must admit I didn't learn a lot. Certainly we were taught to read and write and count to some extent but nothing in great depth. Reading was curtailed by the limited resources and our teacher at the time tried to remedy this by forming a library with pupils bringing in books to lend to others, so to speak. In actual fact, such books often disappeared forever, the thieving lot. I still regret losing my book, The River Pirates.

Grammar was a mystery. We did try, wrestling with terms like *verbs* and *adjectives*, *subject* and *predicate* but we didn't really understand their meaning Later in my education, I even failed to recognise the association with *nominative* and *accusative.* I had by then moved to the 'Big School', the local academy and everything was very strange there. My eyes were opened to a wider world and although I was still having difficulty with my English, this was essentially my spelling ability. When I look back, I really put this down to my accent. I spoke in a very dialectic way common to Southern Ayrshire and so I spelled that way too -according to the sound of the words.

It's not that I dislike English language. I like words. I like their sound, their texture, their feel, their taste, indeed all their various aspects. For this reason I am a slow reader, for I like to savour the character of each word, each syllable. This is what makes reading interesting. We are lucky that we have this wonderful English language full of character and with such a variety of nuances and colour. And when I refer to the English language, I include all its variations that we call dialects. Oh, I know that other languages have their dialects too but nowhere near the same richness and variety.

No doubt we have pinched many of our words from other countries and welcomed them in. I am not aware that we have set up barriers to such inclusion in contrast to France which seems to be jealous of such invasions in an attempt to maintain a pure language. Perhaps we do try to resist Americanisms but without much luck.

I greatly admire poets, those ones who have a feeling for the language and at times invent their own words. They can turn metaphors into words that you can feel and a colour more vivid than the artist or the camera. You can taste the pancake on the griddle or the myrtle's presence on the moorland breeze. The random crookedness of a briar becomes 'All elbows and oxters.' The good poet acknowledges this, uses words accordingly and recognises the music of the word. For music too can be romantic, soulful, threatening. Listen to the soundtrack of the film Psycho, like fingernails down a blackboard. It makes the hairs at the back of your neck stand up.

At school, we had a teacher of English who tried to inculcate in her pupils a feeling for poetry. She tried to test this in the individual by asking each of us to write a limerick. First she had to tell us what a limerick was. I produced this, with the spelling duly corrected:

There was a fair maid from Perth,
Renowned for the size of her girth.
At parties she jiggled,
The others just giggled
And the evening ended in mirth.

She looked at my effort, very closely, and snorted. It was difficult to tell whether or not she approved but let it go anyway. I myself thought it was really brilliant, but that is a biased opinion.

With me, she tried a different tack. "What do you like reading, Kenny?" she asked.

"All sorts of adventure stuff, ghosts and things, and horror things," I ventured.

She sniffed at this, yet had another try. "Have you read any of Edgar Allan Poe," and seeing my blank look, continued, "Here is a copy of *The Raven,* one of his poems. Try writing something like that."

I examined the structure of *The Raven* with a view to producing a version of my own. Here was my effort:

The Budgie

As I lay lolling on my couch of yore with television turned down low,
Methinks I heard a cheeping and a peck, peck, pecking at my
 chamber door.
'Who may that be at this godforsaken hour! a-chapping at my portal,
 making such a din, that chatter peck, peck, pecking!'
That heathenish sound at cocoa time.

Should I go answer this profane, this never-ending peck, peck
 pecking,
This fiendish pecking at the highly polished woodwork, my beloved
 woodwork?
'What diabolic beast are you with wicked beak, a-tap, tap, tapping at
 my highly polished door?'
'Permit me peace at this late Co-co-a hour!'

I slowly rose, reluctant in my hesitation; for Stygian dark and murky
 shadows lurked without, this Advent time.
Suspiring wind moaned round the chimney pots aching for lost souls,
 lost in the ether of the gloom
Where lie in wait all strains of phantom, wraith or bogle, lie in wait
 for me;
And it so near to cocoa time.
With flickering candle I approached the door and laid a fearful hand
 upon a latch so cold.
The door creaked open, inch by wary inch, the candle shivered as wax
 spilled over all my twitching.

Yet all that I could see was blackest night and dancing shadows of the mind.
Back to my chilling stoup of Cocoa.

But there it was again, louder this time, the peck, peck, pecking at the oaken panel of the outer door.
Irate and vexed at this continued interruption of my evening treat, already cooling in my eager hand,
I slammed my cocoa flagon down; I strode and opened wide the creaking barrier to the hostile air,
In flew a flash of green and perched there on the tepid cocoa pot.

The budgie flashed its baleful cocoa-tinctured eye and stared me out full ten or thirteen minutes, maybe more.
Its beak did smile – if beaks can smile – and then began its soulful strain, its ode to me in B flat mine:
'Cheep, cheep' it went and more 'cheep, cheep'; and more and more and more.
'Cheep, cheep' and more; and 'cheep, cheep, cheep' ... and 'cheep' forevermore.

Is there to be no end to such vexatious intervention on such a curséd winter's night as this?
With naught for twilight company but this unnerving passerine, a so-called feathered friend, Kentucky Fried,
Not even that; whose solitary repertoire is but an uninvolved, a cheep, cheep, cheep forevermore,
Settled on my ice-cold beaker's rim, my evening nightcap ruined.

Is this a noble messenger of Gods, Mercury from their gold Acropolis, perchance?

Pray what tidings do you fetch from those far-distant climes beyond
Elysian lands?
Is it my treasure, my estate, my providence? Speak, Herald! What is
there written in the stars?
The budgie turned a Cocoa orb, retorted, 'Cheeky Joey! Who's a
cheeky wee boy, then?'

Teacher's comment: *Not quite what I intended – 6/10*

Thus I entered the mysteries of the great wide world. I left school.

My next stop was in pursuit of knowledge in the ivory towers of a University Arts Department to study English literature. It seems such a wide ranging subject and perhaps it is if you can escape the hobby horse of the professor or the tutor. My problem is that I tend to wander off on my own track and chase my own ideas. I gained an unremarkable masters degree and left to search further gratification in words.

Through various short term jobs in various libraries, I at last settled for a research project into the nature of ancient documents. This took me into the world of calligraphy with its mysteries of colour chemistry and letter shapes. Inevitably this led to the ancient manuscripts of Christian origin with their artistic beauty, books such as the Lindisfarne Gospels and the Book of Kells. Over time, I unearthed the techniques used in the preparation of the original velum, the compositions of the various pigments, their application using egg albumen and the origin of the scripts. Truly, it was the unravelling of a detective story of these ancients.

My real ambition now was to see the original Book of Kells, to see its true glory and somehow to relate to the skill of its originators. It was easier than I thought persuading my boss, Dr Bernard, to foot the bill for my trip to Dublin; and so, all was arranged.

The red-letter day arrived. I was in Dublin and on my way to Trinity College, the home of my enterprise. The library staff members were expecting me and knew of my work in this field; for I had published many papers in the past. They led me to the special air-conditioned room, the realm of the Book of Kells. I gazed in wonder at the precious book, at its glowing and almost writhing contents, and longed to get my hands on the wonder. Of course any handling was out. Yet I could sense the presence of some greater power emanating from the casing.

I asked Emma O'Gary, chief librarian, whether any reproductions were available, in particular, any individual letters for I wanted to examine their structure and artistic composition. She directed my attention to a whole array of postcards and I noticed the high quality of these replicas. I should not have been surprised that the library would cash in on these wonders. I duly selected (and paid for) about a dozen individual single letters and left with my booty to return to my hotel.

In my room I laid the postcards in three rows on the bed so that I could compare one with the other. Some letters were repeated, yet not repeated, for their illumination differed. The creatures, if that is what they were, differed one from the other, perhaps some exotic species of bird to a writhing serpent of the imagination. As I gazed at the cards, their images appeared alive, squirming and writhing this way and that, a dance not of this world. The colours and contours assailed my eyes and thence to my brain until I felt intoxicated by this other-world. A snake like reptile with three bodies had three heads and each head with four sightless eyes. A birdlike beast with a predator's hooked beak had a human profile with cruel lips spewing entrails. And all these creatures tossed and turned, twitched and wriggled in concert to some unheard keening beyond my ears.

I shook my head vigorously to escape this illusion and sat exhausted at the foot of the bed. As for the cards, I hurriedly gathered them and stuffed them into my overnight case.

That night, I slept little, yet when I did I was aware in my dreams of a strange coronach, a very ancient strain mostly like plain chant yet breaking into intervals of fifths. Perhaps long-gone monks, pleased with my appreciation of their work, were praying for me to keep me safe from their demons; or damning me for my interference.

I returned from Dublin and never again looked at those cards, those images, for I jaloused they were not of this world nor of the realms of heaven.

THE ASH GROVE

Recently I had the occasion to recall my early years. At that time, we lived in a small village in Argyll, all in all a self-contained life. It had its own scattering of shops, a post office and even a little teashop. My early education was at the local primary school later followed by a bus journey to the 'big school.' And the reason for the existence of the village? In times long past there had been a blast furnace making pig iron. Only a pile of rubble marks its grave yet there is an extensive wood mainly of ash trees. Originally, the ash trees were coppiced to supply charcoal for the iron process, but that was long ago.

I had a happy childhood in that village with lots of open spaces to roam and many burns to explore and guddle trout. At times during summer, we kids would wander barefooted through the hay stubble, down the hillside and even to the side of the ocean, although perhaps that is stretching the sea loch to its extreme. There was, however, one forbidden place. That was the ash-wooded forest. We were told it was haunted, that it had reek of lost souls. For some reason, I kept clear.

There came a time when those early years became the past and I went out into the wide world and a rose-tinted future. It was a world more complex than I had experienced or indeed had I been prepared for. It was a cruel place where I was denied friendship for I was regarded as a country bumpkin with none of the graces of so-called civilization no matter how hard I tried to adapt. My efforts were regarded with sneers and sometimes hostility.

My work was demanding and, at times, puzzling; for I could see easier methods that were so much more logical and productive only to be rejected or ignored. *What did I know about the business?* Or *What did they teach you with your background?* As you can guess, all this aggression got to me and I just left the office slamming the door. Without a backward glance, I left the building forever.

They tell me that I had something they called 'a nervous breakdown' and I must admit I don't remember a lot of the following days, or weeks, maybe even months. Whatever, I was advised to go back home to 'recuperate', they called it. I called it 'to live again.'

Returning to my home, I realised what I had been missing working in The Big Smoke. Here, I could stretch my eyes to the far away horizon; I could breathe the air and its various fragrances, the peat smoke, the woodbine and other wild flowers; I could wander where the fancy took me. All in all, the sense of liberty was overwhelming.

Unsurprisingly, I was welcomed back to my home and to the whole community. I was back in the familiar surroundings of my former bedroom and I dumped the suitcase of my belongings on the bed. I just sat there and drank it all in.

The room had changed little; the same old chest of drawers,

the one with the sticking drawers forever jamming, placed next the single bed with its candlewick spread; an early picture of mine (aged 7) with stick-men; and, of course, the mirror shedding its distorted reflection. I gazed at myself, good and long, noticing the emergence of worry lines which had appeared since my last visit – when was that? It must be years since my last holiday. I must apologise to my ageing parents for that.

I rooted out my elderly walking boots with a view to exploring some old haunts. Their leather had hardened over the years so I searched out some dubbin and worked hard to soften the hide. It was only then that I thought to check their size. Yes, they fitted, though my feet were tender after years of civilization. After some thought I moderated my ambitious walking programme to a short stroll.

The streets of the village had that same languid air of years gone by. Not much had changed; the shops were all there, even the tearoom; there was a newcomer, a souvenir shop for the tourists. No one was around this mid-afternoon, which wasn't really unusual and I made my way off to explore some past memories, memories of youth; brown trout in the streams; the boulder strewn field of hide and seek; fields of crops waiting for autumn; yet no hay fields to run over. Just as well, for I was in no mood for running. There in the middle distance was the mysteriously forbidden coppiced ash wood. I wondered what mysteries its dark depths hid!

At the evening meal, I stated my intent of exploring the strange wood the following day and I could see the effect on my parents. They looked sideways at one another but said nothing, yet I could detect their uneasiness.

"What's the big mystery of these woods," I asked?

After some hesitation, my mother divulged all, or as much as she knew. Apparently, many years ago, a lass from the village had been wooed by a charcoal burner. In spite of the betrothal, he had abandoned her to the smirks and snide remarks. One day, she had gone into the ash woods searching for her lover never to be seen again, although some say they had noticed strange shadows in the gloomy depths of the undergrowth.

After an uneasy sleep that night, I prepared my hiking gear for the excursion. Not only were my boots feeling the years, my anorak was certainly tighter under the arms, the result of years of soft living. Mother handed a pack of sandwiches with a "Be careful!" and off I stepped with a determined spring to the woodland.

As I approached, I could make out the peculiarities of the trees; for they looked like no ordinary ash trees. As a result of the coppicing, it appeared I was entering an army of inverted umbrellas. These cages of fine branches curving upwards appeared as sentinels guarding access as if to say, "Keep out! Enter at your peril."

Ignoring the warning, I pushed aside the barrier growth of brambles and wild garlic and into the body of the wood. The sunless interior was more open and easier going and there was no difficulty, no further hindrance to my progress. There were no paths to lead me on and so I made a drunken route further into the interior.

By this time, a gentle breeze had risen and blew a kind of wandering tune through the coppiced branches, rather like humming through telephone wires. If I stopped walking and concentrated my thoughts, I imagined I could discern some sort of tune I had still to identify. Through this trackless wilderness I wandered, stumbling across a clearing now and then. There was, to some extent, a great anonymous ambience about the enclosed space, almost claustrophobic. I could feel it getting to me.

For a bit of relief, I stopped in a glade where full light spilled in from a sane outside world. There were even patches of grass and a tree stump to perch on, almost like a picnic site in a layby. That prompted me to produce my sandwiches – my favourite meat roll, that delightful combination of beef and dry-cured bacon cradled in a morning roll.

All this time, the singing trees charmed my brain with their hypnotic song. What was that sense in its ululating refrain? The tune itself bugged me, for its identity dodged around my subconscious. No matter! It would come to me eventually, probably in the middle of the night.

I was becoming more and more relaxed in this unfamiliar atmosphere and began to enjoy its curious ambience. I repacked the remains of my meal and pressed on into the depths. More of the sameness; and I fear for my location. I doubt if I could find the same route out of this maze; but no matter, I had my faithful old compass in my anorak pocket to guide me to the great outside.

On I pushed from glade to shade with all these brolly trees for company and all the time the anonymous melody plagued my mind now rising a semitone as the wind strengthened. Ahead, another break peeped through the trees and I entered a more extensive sward of green. This was different. The sweep of grass was dominated by a king-size ash and from this tree, a brolly of coppice had closed at its upper end to form a cage. As I edged forward, I could just detect something trapped within. I moved forward, closer to get a better view only to recoil in horror as I realised that trapped inside was a skeleton, a human skeleton.

At first I kept my distance, but my curiosity drew me closer for there was no doubt in my mind that these were the sad remains of the deserted lass. There was no clothing to confirm my guess. However, there was a pendant trailing from a vertebra and I could just make out the name "Nell". The arms seemed to embrace the tree so that the two fused together.

I turned away. This was to be my secret and I set to leave the sepulchre of branches undisturbed. It came to me then that I was listening to the tune, that elusive tune, "Through the Wood, Laddie," and I recalled Allan Ramsay's setting,

Though woods now are bonnie, and mornings are clear,
While lav'rocks are singing,
And primroses springing;
Yet nane o' them pleases my eye or my ear,
When through the wood, laddie, ye dinna appear.

ON PROBATION

It was a beautiful funeral. Everyone turned up in their Sunday Best, the men with their custard-spotted black ties which had evidently seen many funeral teas and the ladies with well worn hats, most of them. The singing of the hymns was a bit thin, only to be expected; I put that down to emotion although I could be wrong. The flowers were long lasting and the eulogy short and the coffin interred in due course. Then everyone went off to the Tin Man's Arms for sausage rolls, sandwiches and sweety cakes, I expect. I didn't go, needless to say.

You may have already guessed. Yes! It was my funeral. I think the give-away was the fact that I didn't go to the free nosh-up, so unlike me. Here I am then, all ready to play the ghost while the powers that be decide what to do with me. Anyway, it's certainly better than waiting in that crowded so-called holding room. I should say that, at this stage I'm only a ghost on probation meaning that there are certain things I'm not qualified to do. This includes walking through walls or wailing and various other things.

I've been supplied with some sort of diaphanous covering which would be quite sexy but it obscures nothing. They call the garment *ectoplasm grade D.* I think it is just there for effect. There is an attached label marked with 23X. I suppose that's the size. I have flitted around for a bit just to try out my new outfit and indeed my new prowess at this haunting business. However, I think that this is just a temporary situation. Apparently, you can't just go around groaning and wailing and such like unless you've been murdered, or bricked-up, or beheaded, or something equally bloody – not me, I'm glad to say. I am allowed to move things but not to appear unexpectedly, not yet anyway. I wonder if that means I'm a poltergeist?

I found that ghosts don't go anywhere using some sort of vehicle; nor indeed do they walk. They just need to 'wish a location' and hey presto they've arrived – very environmentally conscious. So I thought, I'll just go and visit my former home, for old times sake – and I was there in an instant.

What was this? There were strangers all over the place. My old house was up for sale? So soon! It was then that I realised that time was a different dimension for ghosts. I could go back and forth as I wished and I seemed to have moved forward by several months. I thought there was something strange and unfamiliar about the place. That's it! Someone had taken the trouble to tidy the house and to clean the various surfaces. The old rambling dwelling looked quite … respectable.

My former house was a small dwelling from the Victorian era, well, small for an old Vic. mansion. Some say that it was designed by Greek Thomson, but I doubt it; for although it had some of the characteristics, it was rather smaller than others of the same era. Nevertheless, it was the sort of ideal place for haunting – plenty of dark corners, narrow passages, creaking floors and groaning doors. I wonder what potential buyers will make of Ayrton Cottage! I'll shadow some of them and eavesdrop, sort of ghosting you might say.

Here is a likely couple, a forlorn husband and a bossy wife. "It looks a bit tired, the decoration and the like," she said. He nodded glumly and I thought, *so would you at that age.* "And that old fireplace would have to come out." What! That's an original Robert Adam. This really is torture. I can't take any more; I'll try another vendor.

Ah! Here is a family group, a young couple with two boisterous boys. They quickly looked around the various rooms and poked among cupboards with not a great deal of interest and I began to wonder if they had just come in to escape the rain. Meanwhile, the two brats were romping around trying out the sturdiness of the furniture. One was flat out on that olive green *chaise longue* that cousin Rachael gave me, whilst the other was bouncing up and down on my Chippendale chair. Oh no! Not the Chippendale! I moved quickly to pull away the chair and as it happened timed it on his downward cycle. The brat landed on his bahouchie with a howl. Exit family, one member blubbing. This haunting business has its moments.

"Oh! Not another one!" I whirled round in ghostly fashion at the sound and there was another one, another ghost. "You are the twenty third one this past while," he went on. To say that I was startled is an understatement. I didn't know my former house was haunted. "Do you have your label?" and he started poking around my ectoplasm. "Ah yes, 23X. I suppose you've come to the right place."

"Should I know you, Mr …?" and my voice trailed away.

"Names don't matter here, 23X. This is merely a transition staging post. I'm here to guide you on to your next stage. I can see that you're merely on probation which means that I have to vet you to see if you are suitable haunting material. Otherwise it's back to the holding room."

Thereafter, he quizzed me about my past – any murders or sudden deaths or anything at all reasonably bloody. Well, I did cut my left ring finger once and it was quite bloody. My mother kissed it better; but apparently that didn't qualify. I really wanted to be licensed to the walking-through-wall phase or maybe just one little wail or a groan, but not even a whimper.

"I really don't see why they sent you here. Perhaps you've poisoned someone," he continued hopefully.

I shook my ectoplasm indignantly for I was quite proud of my cooking ability. I could see that I was getting nowhere at all. "So what happens now? Have I been rejected just as I was getting into the swing of things?"

He hummed and hawed for a bit. "If I send you back to base, you will have to choose."

"Choose? Between what?" I queried.

"Between Paradise and Hades, of course."

"You mean, I have a choice? Tell me more."

My host thought for some time before answering. "Well Paradise is where all is tranquil and peaceful. The air is filled with exotic perfumes and Mantovani strings. The spirits lounge around in placid poses supping the juices of fruits and quaffing the nectar of far-flung flowers. There is no strife, or cross words and all get on with everyone – truly a Paradise."

“And that’s it! – sounds hellish! Are you sure you have things around the correct way? What about Hades?”

“Oh that is where you are sent back to Earth to start another life – from the beginning.”

I’m aghast. That’s no choice at all. “Let me be a ghost … go on, please … please … go on … let me … go on please …”

UNCLE JOE'S TALE

Joe looked in the mirror and reflected. *I've just shaved; it must be Sunday. That's how life goes when you get to my age. You forget the little unimportant things that happen around you – because they are unimportant. All the big things in one's life happened long ago, or so it seems; for those are the things you remember. I can recall the names of my classmates in primary school, but not their faces for some reason. On the other hand, I remember the faces of my classmates in secondary school, but not their names. And so it goes on as I try to recall faces or names from the different phases of my life.*

"Uncle Joe?" He was jolted from his dwam by nephew Charlie, or to be more accurate, his grand nephew Charlie.

"Oh! Hullo there Charlie. I didn't hear you come in. You were going to ask me something, were you?"

"Yeh! Do you believe in ghosts, Uncle Joe," he asked tentatively?

"Why do you ask? Have you just seen one," Joe teased?

Charlie shook his head. "I've been reading about one in this new book I bought yesterday, so I just wondered."

Joe just looked at the 22 year old (or was it 23?) and recalled an event which happened away in the past. "Well, if you like, I'll tell you something that happened to me a long time ago."

Joe continued; "I was maybe 19 or 20 at the time and the family lived in Ayrshire. Do you remember Ayr, quite a bonny place?"

Charlie shook his head.

"Och, I'm sure you do. Don't you remember the sandy shore at Ayr, the sand castles and paddling in the sea? You had a great time there."

"That was 15 years ago, Uncle and isn't that where you rolled up your trousers and put a hanky-with-knots on your head?" he laughed.

"That's the place." Joe shuffled uneasily at the thought. *Trust him to remember the embarrassing moments,* he thought. "Well, we used to live not far from there. The house we lived in was large and ancient, probably from Victorian times. It had the grand title of 'Newfield' or rather 'Newfield Mansion House'. There was an ancient stone with a 1296 inscription set into the wall but I think that was thieved from the local castle. There was something like 30 rooms in the place but we only lived in a part of the building and anyway, it was only temporary until the firm found the family somewhere else."

"The building stood at the top of a small hill and had a view of the distant sea. There was a tennis court with more than its fair share of rabbit burrows and surrounded by a veil of rusty wire netting. The house itself was oblong and plain with rows of anonymous windows. It also had a little tower. One window of the building was different though. That had a green venetian blind. For a time, this puzzled me, for I could find no corresponding window within the building. Eventually I located its position, only to find a blank wall in a large state-room. Apparently, the architect had put the window there to maintain the symmetry of the outside of the house. Apart from that, there was nothing sinister about the place, just a rundown stone building from a bygone era."

"No ghosts then," Charlie cut in.

Joe glared at his nephew. "It was early summer" he went on "and that year, friend Peter and I had planned to go trekking for a week in the wilds of North West Scotland. Since that area was virtually uninhabited, we resolved to take with us all our provisions for the whole period. Since Peter was working in England at the time, it fell to me to plan and collect the food and store it till our departure. That was the morrow."

"That must have weighed a ton," Charley remarked."

"It did, I can tell you. I hurried home to make final preparations. My parents had already gone off to their own holiday destination so I would be undisturbed. The bus let me off at the lane end and I started my tramp to the house. This lane was shorter than the main route, but was a lot more interesting. You entered through the remains of a portico onto an earth-beaten baulk beside a stream, or perhaps it was a ditch. The evening sky had a pinkish/purple hue against the cumulus of storms to come. From a recent shower a legacy of odours lingered, grassy and full of wild garlic mixed with a host of flies. The puddles reflected the pinks of the sky and rippled occasionally with a gentle breeze through the bordering willows. A distant rumble and you could feel the static in the air, the prickling of the skin, the raising of the hair."

"As I quit the lane, I could see before me the dark bulk of the house against a pink sky and its shadow across the tennis court. No welcoming lights or friendly souls disturbed the evening."

"Once inside it was dark before the storm broke; first lightening followed shortly after by transfixing choirs of thunder before the deluge. Torrents of rain rippled across the windows and added to the chorus of noise; but nothing compared to the crack as lightning struck the house and the lights flickered in trepidation. I must say that I was surprised by the strike for I had noticed that there was a lightning conductor down the wall from the little tower. This should have prevented the strike and perhaps it had to some degree. That's science for you! All in all, it had only damaged the wiring with some of the light switches acting erratically. I carried on with my preparations for the morrow."

"I planned to have an early night in anticipation of an early start the following day. With cocoa downed, I tucked myself up for the night with all my trekking gear in the room next door. I should say that the two rooms were only separated by a door; I expect one was a dressing room, at one time a common design in ye olde mansion houses."

"I was restless in bed anticipating the start of the holiday on the morrow. I twisted and turned until I fell into a drowse for a time. A sudden noise roused me; for I could hear something being dragged along the floor of the adjoining room. In an instant I was awake and sat bolt upright. The sound was coming nearer and I could feel the sweat of fear. Whatever it was approached the conjoining door and stopped as did my heart for a moment. Then it started. A knock, knock, knocking.

For a moment, I thought of Edgar Allan Poe, *The Tell-tale Heart* and perhaps the sound is all in my head."

At that point, Uncle Joe drifted off into his dream world. He seemed to be staring into nothing, a faint smile trembled for a moment and Charlie, impatient as ever, sought to drag him back to reality. "What happened next? What did you do?"

"What did I do! I did what any red-bloodied lad of my age would do. I pulled the blankets over my head and spent the rest of the night cowering in a cold sweat."

"But the thing next door, Uncle Joe! What was it?"

"The thing next door! Oh that," said Joe in an offhand way. "That was a mouse. It had found a bar of Aero in my trekking pack and was dragging it to its hole."

"But the knocking. What about the knocking?"

"The chocolate was too large to go in the hole, much as it tried – knock, knock, knocking."

And Uncle Joe just smiled –

And Charlie wondered.

SUDOKU CAN BE DANGEROUS

Joe Cuthbert was a sucker for puzzles, any old puzzle that caught his eye. He would try crosswords, jigsaws, spelling bees, all sorts but his favourite was Sudoku. He would buy book upon book of Sudoku puzzles, you know, the graded kind, and pore over these for hour upon hour. Now that he was retired, he would sit at a table with his puzzles morning noon and night.

Not that he was any good at puzzle solving and Sudoku was no different. Even the most elementary ones would take hours to solve and as he worked through a book, he would reach the 'medium difficult' section and get baffled. At times, this would infuriate Joe and he would pick up the book and throw it into the recycling bin. Nevertheless, he would generally stick to his puzzles for as long at it took.

You could say that Joe had an obsession with Sudoku and he would long for the day when he could solve one from the 'difficult' section. During breakfast he would puzzle long and hard so that breakfast would run into lunch and his porridge would run onto his pullover. Luckily, he lived alone so there was no one to chide him about his table manners. Shirts went the same way as pullovers as indeed did the dining room carpet.

In the middle of one of the medium-difficult Sudoku puzzles, Joe managed to place three identical digits in one large square. Those of you who know the game will recognise that this is against the rules; what's more, to arrive at such a situation must be a talent in itself. Yet there it was, 666 all in a row. At that moment, Joe's doorbell rang.

Grumbling at the interruption, Joe rose to answer the ring.

At the door, there stood a most unusual character in, what might be termed, dated clothes. He was tall and therefore wore his cloak with a certain elegance. This was off-set by a broad brimmed hat calling to mind Sandeman Port, a thought from the past. A deep distinguished voice asked; "Joseph Karriwell Cuthbert? You called my number!"

Joe looked puzzled but went along with the point; anyway, the stranger had his name correct; "Yes! Alright then."

"Don't dither then," the Don continued. "Get your coat and we can start."

With that, the stranger strode off trailing Joe in his wake, in turn trailing his coat behind him. Reaching a black, very shiny car of no make, Joe was ushered onto its rear seat and strapped in by the Don before he placed himself in the neighbouring seat. He tapped the chauffeur's shoulder and they were off.

The car sped through the town centre, past the suburbs and into the countryside. It was an area vaguely familiar yet strange to Joe, becoming more and more bleak as they rolled along. It became even stranger for, in spite of the usual potholes, the car moved smoothly along its route to where … yes, Joe wondered, *where are we going*? For the first time he felt uneasy. Perhaps he should have asked this earlier.

As though reading these thoughts, the stranger stated; "You must be curious about our destination, Mr Cuthbert. There is no mystery. We are going to my home in the country. There we shall wine and dine before proceeding with the Grand Tour." He put added emphases on the last two words.

Tall hedgerows of hawthorn grew on either side blocking the outside world but not the rain, a trickle at first, then an unholy downpour. The swish of the wipers cleared the tunnel ahead and after a ford water-splash, they entered the sweep of a gravel driveway stopping under a stone portico. Light was fading rapidly as evening approached and all had gone to the grey of a wet evening.

Joe was pleased to scramble from the car, through the open door into the warmth of the house, somewhat over warm for that time of year. He crossed a wooden entrance hall with inlaid black-tiled flooring. "Bilé will show you to your room," his host ordered; and with that Joe was led to a stairway up into darkness. His guide opened a door on the second floor to show a sitting room in red leather, indeed in red everywhere.

"Dinner is at seven, sir," Bilé announced and closed the door noiselessly.

Joe wandered across the room touching the furniture with its red leather and unnatural warmth. Heavy rain battered the window as he tried to peer out, yet could discern nothing through the gloom. The darkness kept its secrets well. He explored the room further without reaching any conclusions about the owner. All the time he wondered why he had come to this place. There was no doubt that he felt compelled in some way to join the stranger, yet without any rationale.

His thoughts were interrupted by the bong of a gong, a summons to the meal. Again, he was aware of some strange force drawing him on; *you must obey* it said. Accordingly he descended the dark stairway to a dimly lit door and into the dining chamber. Orange wall lights provided the only illumination until the red candles were lit. The only other occupants were three ladies (a loose description) drably dressed in off-white; they could easily have qualified for the Macbeth play as they huddled together in a corner. Occasionally they would glance in his direction and snigger – or perhaps it was a cackle.

With something akin to a flourish, the host entered through a door at the far end and summoned the others to take their places. The table setting looked sumptuous with its red covering and gold settings. Thirteen red candles provided a glowing centre piece illuminating the faces of those seated round; Don at the head, Joe at the foot and the three wraiths along one long side. It gave Joe his first real opportunity to study the Don. His dark hair was swept back exposing a widow's peak and a high brow. The straight-line contours of his face appeared to slope inwards and down towards his pointed chin. The thin tapering nose accentuated his lined features almost touching the scarlet line of a mouth which could only be described as cruel. The eyes were black coals of bottomlessness, penetrating all before. For the first time, Joe was chilled.

Bilé served the meal, such as it was and Joe noticed that the others ate little. The opener looked like runny porridge and he tasted it with his long handled spoon. Similarly, the main course appeared to be porridge but of a thicker nature. Joe gave the sweet a miss to avoid further porridge. The wine was excellent though and he said as much to his host. The grim host inclined his head in acknowledgement.

Conversation around the table was sparse and trickled away once the condition of the weather was exhausted. "And how do you occupy your time, Mr Cuthbert?" the Don enquired.

"I'm retired now, so I have time to do all sorts," Joe lied. In his mind he felt a little embarrassed about his obsession with puzzles.

"I mean, more specifically," the grim figure pursued.

Joe hesitated, then plunged in, "I do puzzles, solve them, you know, mainly Sudoku."

"That's interesting," his host stated, sounding not in the least interested. "And, are you any good at solving Sudoku?"

Joe shuffled in his seat and sipped wine without answering.

The Dom continued: "You know that it's not Japanese, although the word is. The idea originally emerged in Switzerland in the form of a *Latin square* and was later developed and appeared as a puzzle in 19th century French newspapers before it was known in Japan."

By this time, Joe's eyes were glassy and he just nodded. Just to say something, he remarked, "I wish I was expert at solving Sudoku puzzles. I would give anything to be an expert."

"Even your soul?"

"Yes! Yes, even my soul," he shouted.

The crones cackled and the stranger's mouth twisted ends-up.

* * *

They found Joseph Karriwell Cuthbert at home sprawled over piles of books of Sudoku puzzles, all solved. There were little mounds of porridge all around and a sickly smell in the air. He was twitching and mumbling when they tried to move him and he tried to resist. All at once he screamed: "They are easy, too easy! I can do them all – even the hardest!" They took him away.

Sad to say, he died in hospital two days later still lamenting about these too-easy puzzles.

There had to be an inquest for, in effect his death was a mystery and it was then that the coroner satisfied the curiosity of the masses. His verdict was: Joseph Karriwell Cuthbert – died from an overdose of Sudoku exacerbated by an excess of porridge.

BACKHILL O' THE BUSH

I WAS YOUNG AND THOUGHT I knew everything. I was in love with the great outdoors and thought I knew everything. I enjoyed exploring even to the extent of walking the hills and glens of Scotland on my own; for not only did I think I knew everything, I thought I was invincible.

Thus it was that I planned a winter walk in the wilds of south-west Scotland, an area known as Grey Galloway. Judging from the forecast, the January of that year would be cold but sunny, ideal for hill walking. At that time, the grass would be low, the ground hard with the frost and the walking easy, almost a walk in the park. My aim would be to walk from the south end of Loch Doon and over to about the watershed. There, I would change to a westerly direction and eventually end up in Glen Trool. All pretty vague, you might think, but there are no roads in the area, no A6 or M9, not even a track. So I could not be more specific in my proposed route in my emergency instructions.

Preparations were simple. Pack enough high energy food for three days; my guess was that the venture would take two days and the extra day was for miscalculations – I was vulnerable after all. (I deny that!) The clothing was my usual winter garb: wool jumpers, wool socks, my faithful boots, anorak with hood, sheepskin hat, wool mitts, goggles. My equipment was somewhat basic: compass, map, knife-on-lanyard, walking pole, tent, sleeping bag, solid fuel stove all packed away in my rucksack. The map, compass and knife I kept handy in my kangaroo pouch.

I don't know if you are familiar with this part of Galloway. It has changed considerably since the days of my hillwalking, for much of it has been planted with pine. There is even a charge to enter the castle there; that is the one which was removed from its island and rebuilt on the shore because of the hydro scheme. There is even a caravan park further along.

It was a much more desolate place in those faraway days. Then, the castle was certainly on the shore, whereas the area was one vast moorland hemmed in by the Rhinns of Kells to the east and Benyellary/Merrick in the other quarter. Two rivers, the Gala Lane and the Eglin Lane flow into the south end of the loch. It was there that I intended starting my journey.

All clad for the cold weather and my rucksack on my back, I made off southwards along the valley of the two rivers and after a bit, I stuck with the Gala Lane. I kept well away from the rivers though, for walking there was difficult because of the frequent flooding. Great grass tussocks stuck up proud by about a foot from a muddy base trapping unwary boots or tripping unwary walkers. It was easier to follow one of the many sheep tracks.

Soon sweat ran down from a puzzled brow. Where was all the frost-hardened ground? It was decidedly soggy and hard work. A darkness was gathering to the south and the reason for the mild weather soon became apparent. Large flakes of snow drifted down, settled on my eyelashes and made my route uncertain. It was time for my goggles and a compass fixed to my wrist. With the snow cloud thickening, I was totally dependent on my compass, for now it was total whiteout. As for me, I must have taken on the appearance of an abominable snowman.

On I plodded into this unknown cloud of snow, generally keeping a southerly course. I feared I would have to camp somewhere till this weather passed and with this in mind, I started looking for a sheltered spot, a large rock perhaps to pitch my tent in its lea. Where have all the rocks gone? The white of the snow blotted out the features of this barren land. I stopped, turned my back on the weather and rested with a high-energy bar – or so it says on the wrapper.

Time to move on and I continued into the blizzard, for it was a blizzard by now. The going didn't seem so difficult and I guessed that I had reached the watershed. The sky darkened further, for the day was short and although I thought I was near the bothy, there was no way I would find it in this whiteout. Over a rushing stream and onward in the failing light.

Ghosts of snow danced around my slow progress, seeming to mock me in my puny efforts against the storm. Snow caked my garments and sometimes blinded my goggles before I sent it scattering. The ground under my boots was rocky and uneven twisting my feet this way and that. Sometimes I staggered and once I had occasion to sit down as the rucksack pulled me off balance. There was a sudden fall in the wind and there through a snow curtain, I thought I caught a glimpse of a light. I took a quick fix with my compass before the wind closed the snow curtain.

Keeping close to this bearing, my direction was more positive. Crossing another stream and there was my saviour, my delivering light sent forth from a building. Nearer and there was the bothy, the Backhill o' the Bush.

I entered by the porch and stamped most of the snow from my boots. A similar shake of my anorak cleared it as I entered left into the main room; "Hullo, it's only me, the snowman." There on a low stool sat a man cradling a well-worn briar pipe. He merely grunted in reply. I edged closer to the glowing stove, eyeing the other. Lit by a single tallow candle, he had the appearance of a man of the hills. His weathered complexion hid his age, well over middle-aged, I guessed and his blue eyes seem to be focused on ten miles away. He stood up a full six feet and offered his hand in greeting – a good strong grip. His tweeds were well used, wool socks of course, and heavy duty working boots. Perhaps he was a shepherd and this was his place, such as it was. I didn't think so, for the inside seemed a bit rundown. Certainly the walls were lined with pine tongue-and-groove, yet I noticed in passing that a neighbouring room had lost much of its wood, fuel for the fire, no doubt.

"I'm Tam Shepherd," he stated in a gravelly voice well used for calling his dogs. I have decided he must be a shepherd, judging by his name and that this must be the centre of his herding operations.

I ventured, "There is a wee shop in Queen Street, Glasgow by the same name …"

"No relation," he interrupted gruffly. He had probably been asked the same many times.

I returned to warming up with some cocoa and I planned my evening meal. Tam returned to puffing his briar using a splint of wood to rekindle. "Do you fancy some cocoa?" I asked; yet he only shook his head and continued puffing.

I pressed on with my meal, essentially a tin of sausage and baked beans on top of a morning roll followed by an apple. The heat of the stove was inviting and I could fain have dropped off there and then. Yet I felt that that would be rude, despite the lack of conversation.

"Whar dae ye bide, laddie?" he asked breaking his reticence at last.

"I live in Ayr. I'm just up here for a bit of a break – walking the hills – getting a bit of exercise, like. I've walked here from the end of Loch Doon," I bragged.

Tam nodded his head. "You'll be on yer way tae Carsphairn, then laddie?"

"Maybe later. I fancied walking over to Loch Enoch and then maybe up the Merrick, if the weather settles, Mr Shepherd."

"Och, just ca' me Tam, laddie." (I wish he would drop the 'laddie' bit. It makes me out to be a kid.) "Mind your way across the Silver Flowe, a treacherous bit o' land. Mony a guid chiel has been lost there trying tae rescue a sheep. Aye, richt treacherous, laddie! Mind you, it'll be frozen wi' the recent cauld, sheer hard." He puffed away at his pipe for a bit.

"Whatever ye dae, dinna gang near the Murder Hole, though. An evil place that, a' can tell ye. Evil! Loch Enoch is a'richt though. Did ye ken that the trout there have their tail fin worn awa'. They say it's because o' the white sand, really coarse it is. Whiles they use it tae sharpen knives and gullies and the likes – scythes tae."

So, he went on extolling the virtues of the place, then again, "Dinna gang near the Murder Hole, laddie," as I climbed the stairs to the attic.

By the light of my torch, I rolled out my sleeping bag and snuggled in fully dressed. I could feel the cold closing in and a few snow flakes wandered through the broken skylight. Up again to stuff the hole with some hay. Back in my bag, I tossed and turned as I thought of the evening's conversation. At first I thought I was restless because of the tobacco smoke, yet that didn't bother me, not in the same way as my grandpa's pipe. Mind you, grandpa smoked either Bogey Roll (self cut) or Warlock, both mighty powerful. I didn't recognise Tam's blend at all; indeed, I didn't even remember smelling it. More tossing and turning and I came to the conclusion that a rucksack doesn't make a good pillow.

Up fine and early the next morning; it was just light and I could see a clear sky through the cracked skylight. I decided that I would tackle the walk west to the Merrick. Hurrying down stairs, I found no sign of last night's companion and guessed he had work to do elsewhere.

It was easy-walking towards Mulwharcher and before I knew it, I was stepping onto the Silver Flowe. Not that you'd notice its treachery, for it had frozen solid and presented no problems. Loch Enoch was frozen too and there was snow everywhere. As for the dreaded Murder Hole, there was no sign of it anywhere; nor could I find it on the map. There was certainly a Fairy Ring marked. Maybe it had had a name change.

Later, retracing my route back to the bothy, I could see a light from its window. Perhaps Tam was back and was good enough to light the stove. Yet no! It was merely the refection of the setting sun and there was no Tam, no fire, just a freezing cold Backhill o' the Bush and I had to set the fire myself.

It was a quiet meal that evening and I longed for the company and the pipe of the mystery friend. With little else to do for the rest of the evening, I decided to bed down in front of the stove. I don't think I could face the arctic loft again.

The following morning after a quick breakfast in the frigid room (the stove had gone out) I packed my gear and bade farewell to the Backhill o' the Bush. My route took me over the Rhinns near Millfire and eventually to a tarmac road. Down this road was the sanctuary of Carsphairn and a snug little pub. It was dark when I reached my destination where there was no difficulty getting bed and breakfast; there were no other travellers crazy enough to be walking the cold, cold hills in this weather.

Later in the crowded bar, I seemed to be the centre of attention since I was the only stranger there. We talked about this and that, and Jimmy who I vaguely knew from the distant past asked about my walk. "So where did you get to this time?"

"I came down from Loch Doon in the snow and the next day I had a great walk over to Loch Enoch across the Flowe," and sipped my lager. "Spent a couple of nights in Backhill o' the Bush."

"The old bothy? Did you come across the ghost of the bothy, then?" He saw my startled look and pressed, "Ye met Auld Tam?"

I nodded.

"Did ye hear that, lads? He met Auld Tam of Backhill o' the Bush, the one that's supposed to have died in the Murder Hole."

And I had free drinks for the rest of the evening.

THE UNAUTHORIZED VERSION

I WAS ONCE ASKED WHERE I would go if I had the choice of anywhere. Anywhere? Really anywhere? What a choice to make. Let me think now. There are all these romantic places along the Mediterranean. Och no! Everyone goes there – too crowded, although there is the Fountain of Youth; Naw! I'm a bit past that, I should think – beyond redemption, they say. Perhaps a journey to the stars, the ones in the heavens but that would have to be limited; for the nearest, Centaurus is about 5 light years away and would therefore take at least 5 years at the speed of light. I'm not prepared to spend 5 years sitting in a space craft. I would die of boredom and anyway, at the speed of light doesn't matter turn to energy and I would burn up.

I think I'll stick to Scotland. Uncle Hamish Macleod, really a grand uncle on my mother's side, once told me a tale which lived with him for the rest of his days.

It was in the year 1900 when he was fishing from Stornoway on the Island of Lewis. He had a Seine netting boat, Fair Wind, clinker built and as sea-worthy as any vessel sailing from the Western Isles. The sister boat, Golden Harvest, was the other part of the fishing partnership and being Seine netting boats, they worked in pairs. It was part of that fishing technique and was particularly successful in catching herring.

Uncle Hamish's Tale

The fishing was good that year but it was getting on and Christmas was not all that far away. There had been a recent violent storm out of the west that had kept me in port and any fish in the Minch were being shy for the past two weeks. I remember that it must have been a Thursday, for the Harbour Bar was conveniently open. Golden Harvest *had just tied up and skipper, Geordie McLean came through the swing doors. We greeted each other like the old pals that we were. 'Hamish,' he said as he had a deoch of the local brew, 'I've just come frae the Seven Hunters direction and, dae ye ken, there's nae light frae Flannan; nor could I see any action around the lighthouse. I fear there's something not right there. I would have landed but for the tail sea running.'*

I could understand his reluctance to go too near the Seven Hunters, for these are treacherous waters and many a vessel had foundered there before Stevenson's lighthouse. If I don't do something, I thought, there will be another wreck on the Seven Hunters.

It would be dusk shortly so I went searching for Wee Jimmy, one of my crew and we prepared Fair Wind *for the voyage, checked the fuel and lit the blow lamp to heat the hot bulb above the cylinder for starting. Chugging away, we made for the Butt before taking her dead West into the teeth of the swell. The worst of the storm had gone but there was still quite a sea running making the journey a wet one. Every now and then, the prow of the boat would dig into a rogue sea sending green water over the deck, so the two of us spent most of the time sheltering in the tiny cuddy.*

Night came early, as it does there in December and the glow of the navigation lights lit our faces, red on mine and green on Jimmy's. Heavy spray tattooed the windscreen distorting the scene forrard like those modern bubble-glass windows I keep hearing about and it was just into morning light before the Seven Hunters appeared on the horizon. I took the boat into the eastern lea of Eilean Mor as close as I dared, dropped the hook and we launched the tender.

This took us to the east landing stage where we tied up and the both of us scrambled up the wet cement-way to the lighthouse door.

We chapped on the door of the keepers' house and entered the tiny building. Where was everybody? Over at the tower, Jimmy climbed the spiral stair to both levels. I could hear his progress, echoing steps rebounding from the bare stone walls. "Here Skipper, up at the light." It was Jimmy calling. When I reached the light platform, there was Donald, all thrawn and white, staring into space with a pale-faced Jimmy kneeling. "What's happened, Donald? Where are the other two?" But there was no response. I turned to Jimmy: "Let's get him out of here and into the boat afore the seas get us;' and we half dragged, half carried Donald down the stairway and onto the ramp. With the lighthouse keeper in the tender we rowed back to Fair Wind *and sanctity.*

The boat's engine was warm enough to restart and without delay, I took a course back to Lewis. There was a feeling of disquiet behind us and I felt no urge to linger. The sea was still running hard with giants all the way from the Americas. We would climb one monster and surf down the other side, an experience normally exhilarating, but there was no pleasure that day. Nor was there any response from the lighthouse keeper on the way back to Stornoway. With the sea on our stern and a tail wind, we soon saw the white flash of the Butt light and we managed the rest of the journey in daylight, for there was the white flash at Arnish point.

Back in port, we had a struggle getting Donald up the quay steps and along the street to Jessie Mackenzie's place. She would know how to look after him.

"But wait a minute, Uncle Hamish. I thought all three keepers vanished, " I exclaimed. According to the papers at the time, all three disappeared." Uncle Hamish just smiled, looked at his pipe and started cutting fresh tobacco from a Bogy Role.

* * *

Yes! That's where I'd like to go – the Flannan Islands.

TWA CRAWS

It was only last year that I took up this job for a magazine. It was a sort of survey involving cataloguing details and location of brass ornamentations on tombs in the various churches, cathedrals and other holy sites throughout England. Not that I was particularly interested in brass rubbing as such, but I was short of employment - and cash – at the time. I still am when I think about it.

The job was interesting enough as it took me all over the country and into some dark corners of the hallowed world. Such tombs were often located in dark and sometimes rather spooky corners yet I soon became accustomed to such atmospheres. I would often be seen lurking around such dark nooks, my LED light strapped to my head, my recorder for note taking slung around my neck and my tiny radio-mike in my left hand.

On this occasion, I was scrambling around this medieval church near Morpeth in Northumberland, when I came across this double tomb tucked away in one corner. It was the last resting place of two warriors, or rather two knights, by name Sir Francis de Ravencross and Sir Charles de Ravencross. They both had brass plates detailing their exploits against the marauding border Scots yet these lacked any precision such as battles or the like. The brass likenesses of the two were not the usual three-dimensional image; rather they were flat brass plates with engraved representations.

I duly dictated the details in my recorder, their dates and life spans, and in stretching to examine an armour detail on one of the brasses, I slipped and dropped my microphone. Down it clattered and bounced away, I know not where. I searched around the stone floor, its crevices and nooks and crannies and came to the conclusion that it had escaped down one of the floor gratings. It certainly was small enough.

Using my head torch, I peered through the grating but could only detect the dusty detritus of past centuries – no radio mike. As I couldn't afford to just leave it there, I pulled and tugged at the grating. It wouldn't budge – of course not. The grating was bolted to the floor and expected to stay there for the next century or two.

After a few moments, I decided to find out if there was a caretaker around. After all, that's what they were there for, to help people in crisis, if you can call it that. Leaving my recorder and gear, I went searching for a warden or curator or someone to help. I eventually succeeded in locating the building's antiquities warden and led him to my problem. He suggested I use a spanner to loosen the holding bolts; it was not going to be an easy task. "These two are forever causing problems," he remarked. "We call them The Twa Craws." He didn't elaborate.

Rummaging around the chaotic boot of my car, I found a selection of box spanners and some WD 40. Believe it or not, the grating bolts turned easily enough and I was able to search the darkness below, odd scraps of paper, even Polo Mints and dust, mainly dust. Poking around the two stone cists, the last resting places of Francis and Charles, I hit the jackpot. Yes! Here it was, my radio mike partially tucked under one of the stone coffins.

With everything back in place, I picked up my gear with every intention of continuing my survey. Another setback! I had left my recorder running and it had run out of memory. I had no option then but to give up for the day, return to my hotel and analyse the data already on the disc.

With the recorder on the bed, I sat on the only chair in the room and pressed *Playback*. Yes. There were my observations about the two brasses – no problem. Then the moment when the mike jumped from my hand – yes, I declare that it deliberately jumped – followed by an expletive or two unbecoming for a holy place. About to press *stop* I hesitated for I was sure that I heard another voice. I ran the recording back and replayed that section with the volume turned up fully. Yes, there was a voice, indeed two, speaking in a strange accent. This conversation continued for some time in this odd accent and it was only later that I managed to decipher this dialogue.

I wrote down this exchange as best I could and tried to assign the various parts to the two separate voices. Early on, it was pretty evident that one voice was Charles and the other Francis and, after some juggling and amendments, I arrived at this final version. This is penned below, though I should say that there are no World shattering revelations. I have tried to express their words in a modern idiom.

What was that, Fran?

Nothing much, Charlie; another mint, I think.

You think! Can't you be sure, Twisted Neb? Find out ye wastrel.

Listen, Pudding Face, I wish you wouldn't keep referring to my nose like that. You know fine it was an accident with my visor. Anyway, you can talk. You fell from your horse at Coldstream and were taken by the Armstrongs. A pretty penny we had to pay to get you back – and your armour was bashed useless by the fall. It took the Armstrongs hours to get you out – and they were laughing for hours after. I felt humiliated when I had to fetch you.

How do you think I felt, Nebby? And it was supposed to be top-grade armour. Anyway you can talk, you blackguard. We had to ransom you when you were unseated that time at Kelso and had your thumb caught in your stirrup. It was the MacFarlanes that time.

That was jolly painful, ye varlet and they had to cut it off to free me.

And so it went on like this, on and on, a typical family feud for those days. Eventually it boiled down to Charles had to be ransomed three times and Francis twice all due to ineptitude in the saddle or cheap and faulty armour, ex-army surplus I expect. It all ended with

Why did I have to be interred with this knave of a brother!

Why indeed, you rapscallion!

and both going into a huff, refusing to speak.

Next day, on checking with the antiquities warden, I find that both went down in history as two impeccably brave warriors, fighting side by side and eventually dying peacefully in their beds.

I didn't disillusion him.

BERTIE

When I was a student – long enough since, to tax the memory – cash was forever short. It follows that any long periods of leisure were taken up with short-term jobs. Thus, it happened that one June, I started working in a brickworks essentially doing odd labouring jobs filling in if one of the others was off. In this way, I covered many of the tasks in this industry. Certain tasks were barred mainly because I didn't have the relevant skills. Controlling the clay/water mix took years of experience and firing the kilns required years of know-how. Nor was I permitted to empty the kilns – timmers they were called – for this was a much coveted job being paid as piece work. Anyway, I didn't hanker after the oppressively hot conditions nor the razor-sharp edges of the bricks tearing my hands to shreds.

The brickworks was set in its own site right next to the local coal mine, the source of its raw material, a sort of blue, carbon-rich clay. The kiln was a Hoffmann (tunnel version) with 24 chambers surrounded by a rail system. There was a tiny edifice (a sort of cuddy) built on top at one corner and over there was the typical square-shaped chimney set at a short distance. The manufacturing machinery shed was sited beyond and near the coalmine. There was also a small Newcastle kiln of three chambers but I never saw it used. Essentially, it provided storage for spare machinery.

On the face of it, the Hoffmann kiln used a simple system for continuous operation. The chambers were arranged in two rows, side by side and through the operation of dampers, the hot fire region would progress along one row and then up the other. In effect, it was a continuous, cyclic progression. In front of the hot region, the setters would build a pattern of raw blue-clay bricks fresh from the machine, whereas the timmers would follow the hot front and cart away the finished product.

It was a dirty job. The very nature of the activity involved dust and dirt. Essentially, shale from the local coal mine was finely ground, mixed with water and compressed into brick shapes. These were set in a kiln, fired for a period and allowed to cool before shipping off by lorry to some builders merchant. It was actually more complex than that but that essentially was it. The plant was ancient, probably Victorian, and noisy – very noisy, so much so that normal conversation was impossible and intentions were conveyed by signs, sometimes very rude ones.

In such situations where a relatively small work force was used, each individual knew all about the other and indeed I still remember them well after many, many years. Their names have disappeared into history but their faces are still there. One in particular stands out and I *do* remember that his name was Bertie.

Now Bertie was, what you would call, simple. Although the others teased him to some extent, it was in the kindest way. For generally, I think the men were fond of and protective towards

Bertie. One instance comes to mind when during a general election, Bertie, a staunch Tory, voted Labour by mistake – laughter all round much to his dismay. Nonetheless, they would have laughed had any of them made such a blunder.

Bertie's appearance was unusual. He looked as though he had no top teeth and so his bottom jaw seemed to jut out. He wore a hat which I feel he designed himself. Originally it had been a soft hat but he had cut the brim away to leave the front part as a sort of skip. It was certainly unique. He glared out at the world from under this skip, it seemed with a hostile air although I suspect it was in puzzlement. Each evening, he would leave the works on his bike covered from head to foot in dust and grime. Bertie was the odd job man.

Ashes had to be removed regularly from the kiln. The pan mill would break down and dusty, ground clay had to be shovelled down a chute from the stoorie loft – it wasn't called "the stoorie loft" for nothing. Constantly, drossy coal as fuel had to be barrowed to the kiln top. Bertie was your man.

Bertie always regarded me with suspicion on the strength of the boss being my father. No doubt the others had been filling his head with all sorts of nonsense related to this and that had made him wary. In any case, I just went about my daily tasks like the others and we had no occasion to concern one another. Nonetheless, it did bother me. I felt I had to communicate with him on some level. I don't know why.

The first few weeks of the job continued in this fashion and workers came and workers left; for there was constant movement in the labour market of the brick trade due, no doubt, to the dirty work and the poor pay. One Monday there was a new arrival in the form of one, Karl Johnston – nicknamed Basher. He was a large thickset individual with a loud mouth. You could see from the beginning that he was trouble. He was forceful in manner and voice and he let everyone know how tough he was. And who were we to doubt it.

For some reason, or no reason at all, Basher took a dislike to Bertie. He would harass Bertie, addressing him in the most derogatory terms and I could see that the others didn't like that but said nothing. On one occasion, big Jan, the Pole, had to be restrained which is just as well; for both would have lost their jobs had there been any fighting. Even the foreman said nothing. Thus it continued day after day and meal breaks were no pleasure, no crack, no jokes.

The whole affair came to a head one day, towards the end of a shift. I was wheeling a barrow along the track to the far end of the kiln and well away from the noise of the machinery when I heard this bong, like a gong being bonged. It came from just round the corner and I hurried forward. Did I say, "Came to a head"? It certainly had! There, round the corner, stood Bertie with a spade in one hand and Basher at his feet. He had an unnatural dent in his head. Blood was flowing along with some yellowish liquid which I guess was brain matter. The spade was one of those heavy ones with the business end shaped like a playing card spade. Basher was in no shape at all. He was dead.

"He ca'd ma mither names," mumbled Bertie.

I looked at Bertie, Bertie stared at Basher and Basher stared at nothing with a blankness that was disturbing. I had to do something. "Quick, Bertie. Get him into the barrow and we'll dump him into the sump under the chimney."

Between us, we lifted the body into the barrow and Bertie wheeled him the short distance to the chimney without being spotted. There, we opened the hatch to the sump and could see the reflection of water there. It was rippled by the surge of draft through the open hatch interrupted by the splash as we dumped the body. The hatch sucked shut as we closed it and we returned to the refuge of the kiln wall.

"Now, listen here Bertie! We've got to get rid of this body. Anyone clearing out that sump is going to find Basher."

Bertie just looked at me with the same old blank expression and I couldn't see any ideas coming from him. I had an idea though; a plan was crystallizing in my mind. It just needed a little bit of effort from both of us. It was getting near the end of the shift and Basher's empty bogie had still to be returned to the machine shed and a full one collected for the setters. "Bertie! Take the bogie back and I'll think of something."

Once he had gone, I started doing some calculations and reckoned my plan might just work.

Bertie returned with the last bricks of the day and pushed the bogie into the setters' chamber. It was lousing time and everyone was preparing to leave.

"Berty! A word before you go," and I cornered him as he came from the chamber. "You know, you are in a serious situation here," and he nodded, the first indication that he understood the plight. "We'll return tonight and put things right, or as right as they'll ever be. Meet me tonight back here at eight … no, not here. Meet me by those trees by the gate and come on your bike. Remember! Eight o'clock at the trees." And he nodded again.

* * *

I cleaned myself up and managed to arrive early. Bertie beat me to the rendezvous and stood there shaking slightly. I didn't want to enter the works site too early and dusk was just settling in. I thought I'd better outline the plan rather than just hang around; for two people in conversation would look less suspicious to the casual passer-by.

As night approached, the works' operating lights came on. I had forgotten all about the lighting system. It was there to guide the stoker around the kiln top during his firing job and was in no way a security precaution. We would wait till he returned to his bothy and then approach from the blind side. We could see him now raising the cups one by one and scooping coal into each. In five minutes, he had finished and returned to his refuge.

"Leave your bike in the bushes and follow me – and keep quiet, Bertie!"

We reached the shadow of the kiln and made our way round to the chimney end. The light spilled out and showed the sump hatch, our first destination. "When I open the hatch, you jump down and lift him. I'll grab from this end."

The body was even heavier than before, for the water in the sump had soaked into his clothing. Puffing and panting, we laid him on the gravel and quickly closed the hatch before the stoker noticed the change in the draught. "Quick! Leave him there and get behind the stack. Jimmy's coming out again to stoke. He'll no' notice basher. The lights'll blind him."

Moving the body is going to be a problem. He is so much heavier than I anticipated. There is that barrow propped against the kiln wall. We'll use that. When the coast was clear, I quickly dashed, grabbed the barrow and wheeled it back to the chimney. There we loaded the body and quickly wheeled it over to the kiln and into the chamber where the setters had been working earlier. The body was tipped onto the ash floor.

It was dark inside the kiln with only a little overspill from the lights above. I had the foresight to bring a candle with me but it showed little in that spacious chamber. "Go and fetch your torch from the bike, Bertie. Be careful Jimmy doesn't see you and try to be quiet." Off he went, glad to get out of the place, I expect. It was beginning to smell in the residual heat of the tomb-to-be.

By the dim light, I examined the wall of blue/green unfired bricks and noted the setting pattern and the number of bricks in one width. This gave me the midpoint of the wall marking it with a line in the ash. Just then, Bertie arrived back with his torch.

"What we're going to do is take down these two brick courses up to this halfway line and start rebuilding them into a new course in front of the left half. The two missing courses should give us plenty of room to hide the body. Just extend that new course right along to complete the hiding place."

And so it was as we laboured through the night and completed the job. It was probably two in the morning as we shared the last of a bottle of Irn Bru. Time to get out.

Bertie gave me a ride on the bar of his bike to the main road two miles away and I walked the rest of the way home. It was only then that the enormity of our deed struck me and I trembled violently as I lay sleepless in bed.

* * *

Next day at 7am, it was back to work and as luck would have it, there were two absentees – one being Basher of course. I was put onto setting along with Jan, the Pole and Bertie on to pushing bogies with green brick. That should keep us away from thinking of the previous evening's events. Not a bit of it.

There was I in front of a dyke one brick-course away from the body. Perhaps not a bad thing, for any fault in our previous night's work would go unnoticed. I started the morning's labour willingly enough until Jan remarked, "It smells like someone died in here."

I quickly looked round and with a tremor, "Aye. Someone's been using the place as a toilet," I remarked and let it go at that.

I could see that Bertie was going to be a bit of a problem for he refused to push the bogie into the chamber. However Jan just took this as his normal behaviour and the two of us manhandled the trolley along the floor plate.

Thereafter, the morning passed without incident and by nightfall, the chamber was complete and we had moved onto the next one.

By the weekend, all passed without any further drama. That was kept till the following week.

On the Tuesday, a police car pulled into the yard and two officers got out. I could see that Bertie was getting jittery and was eyeing his bicycle. I got to him before he actually took off and managed to calm him.

"I'll try and find what's happening, Bertie," and I edged

close to Eddie, the foreman who had turned out of his office. My excuse was a request for more paint for a job I was on.

"We're looking for a Mr Johnston," one of the officers began, "a Charles Johnston. I believe he works here?"

Eddie scratched his head and looked puzzled. Then it dawned. "Oh, you mean Karl Johnston. Oh, we haven't seen him since … wait till I check," and he re-entered his office. "Yes," he called from the door, "last Tuesday. We haven't seen him since last Tuesday."

The officer didn't seem surprised. "He was due in court yesterday and didn't appear … jumped bail … assault charge. Thanks anyway," and with that, the two policemen drove off.

Ironically, their departure coincided with Basher's, or rather his cremation; for the hot front had just reached that chamber.

CALAMITY JIM

Sometimes I ask myself why I made chemistry my profession, not pharmacy but real chemistry, the stuff of big bangs or rank smells, bright colours or tough fibres. Perhaps it was the early experiences when chemistry seemed like magic, for magic or conjuring was one of my earlier delights.

The magic of chemistry became evident in my secondary school days. It was then I encountered the idea that certain things changed their form when mixed with other things. When I took some nice blue copper sulphate in water and added a drop to this, just a drop, of ammonia in water, the nice blue changed to inky dark blue. It was magic. Or phenolphthalein in water, a wine colour, magically turned colourless with the addition of a drop of acid; almost like wine turning to water, the basis of an old trick. There is an abundance of 'tricks' like this.

Big bangs are a different matter and I try to avoid these. The trouble with bangs is that they are often accompanied by heat or flying missiles. My first encounter with a bang was a deliberate experimental one in school. A balloon was inflated with a mixture of hydrogen and oxygen (2/1 mixture), taken on a long pole into the playground and ignited with a lighted cigarette – a very impressive bang. It's probably not done these days what with health and safety together with smoking bans, which is a pity; for it rather drives home the dangers of bangs. There was another bang (in those early days) when a teacher went looking for a gas leak with a lighted taper, but that's another story.

Even when I progressed to university, there were bangs, all part of the scene. I recall one lecturer demonstrating the production of hydrogen using acid (hydrochloric, I think) and zinc metal in a sturdy piece of equipment called a Kipp's Apparatus (after the LATE Petrus Jacobus Kipp). To test that all the air was expelled, he touched the end with a lighted taper expecting to see a benign hydrogen flame. Instead, there was a very loud bang and the apparatus disappeared in a shower of glass fragments. He received a tumultuous round of applause. So much for health and safety, unheard of at that time.

When I moved into industry, the test-tubes were bigger which meant that the bangs were too. After all, I was no longer using grams but tons or rather, metric tonnes. If the works' site had a building with no roof, then there was a reason, usually a bang. I have worked on such a site, but again, that's yet another story.

On one site I worked, a bang was a sign that a safety device had worked. My part of the process was the purification of the ethylene before it was piped next door to the polyethylene plant. Essentially, my plant had to remove or transform any stray acetylenes using a catalyst; for they were a problem when compressed to the very high pressures of the polyethylene plant and caused the process to run out of control. The resultant sudden pressure increase would cause the weakest part to explode. However, the plant was designed to anticipate this and deliberately incorporated a weak point in the form of a bursting disc. So we, on one side of the fence would hear a boom and about ten minutes later polyethylene snow would fall – very Christmassy.

For my next project, I was transferred to another group under a certain James Galloway, an unknown quantity as far as I was concerned. Over lunch one day, I asked some friends about him just as a sort of preparation.

Friend Frank chuckled. "Don't you know Jim?" he exclaimed. "He's generally known as Calamity Jim." Then he set out to put me in the picture.

"The first I heard the name, Jim was in the process of testing a rotary kiln to be used in the calcining of anhydrite, a form of limestone. This process heats the kiln to about 1500C which suited Jim. He liked working on the edge; I think it gave him a thrill. All went well. The kiln rotated, the temperature rose, the anhydrite was fed in, the clinker exited. Lunchtime came, all was shut down and everyone drifted off to eat. Well, the kiln being very hot and not rotating was his undoing. When they returned after about an hour, the kiln had sagged around the middle which meant it was useless and ended up in the scrap-yard. An expensive experiment."

"Tell him about the granulator," interrupted Ronnie.

"Oh yes! There was the thing with this granulator," Frank continued.

I looked at Frank with question marks.

Frank went on,"Jim had this project going using a granulator to make fine granules of fertilizer. This was before we built the prilling tower, you understand. He arranged feed in at one end of the rotating granulator expecting grains of fertilizer from the other end. He used too much water to hurry the process along – impetuous as ever. What he got was one very large ball dropping from the end. He thought about this overnight, which was a mistake. The remaining material set inside the unit like cement and it took a squad the whole week to chip out."

"And then there was …"

"Hold on, hold on you lot! You're just trying to give me the heebie-jeebies.

Let's just leave it at that." My two companions just grinned at each other, their ploy complete. Nevertheless, it was with some reservation that I joined Jim Galloway the following week.

Jim greeted me with some enthusiasm and got into the business of the day. His project concerned the design of stacks[4] or rather the ignition system, to be more exact. I didn't like the sound of that. I should explain that stacks were used to burn-off gas that is out of specification, but of course it has to be lit usually by a pilot light (just like some old domestic gas stoves). The project concerned this pilot light.

He explained; "It used to be the practice to send someone up the ladder with a large flaming torch, just to light the pilot light."

I just looked at him and thought of his reputation. "Oh yes?" (and I thought "Oh yes!")

---

4. A stack is a term used for a chimney.

"How are you with heights?" and I thought I could detect a twinkle in his eye.

Not to be fazed, I declared, "Alright, I suppose. I've done a bit of rock climbing though I can't say I've ever climbed a stack," anticipating his follow-up. "In any case, isn't that a job for a steeplejack? I don't wish to cause a strike."

"We in research department don't need to use union labour for our little experiments," Jim declared and I let it go at that.

Over the following couple of weeks, we worked on the design of this new ignition system and came up with an ugly looking contraption of tubes and wires. A single wire would run from the device down the full height of the chimney and the brass attachment to the metal stack would provide an earth. So much for theory!

Came the day when Galloway turned to me. "Up you go then – and when you get there, screw this ring to the small threaded tube next to the stack. Here, wear this harness and clip onto the fixed ladder as you go up."

I donned the climbing harness, gazed at the ladder and clipped his strange device to my belt. The ladder seemed sound enough and the series of hoops to the top would give some sense of security. Up I climbed.

Rung after rung I climbed the ladder. There was a gentle breeze around and for a time it kept me cool. Nevertheless I was beginning to feel the exertion and I stopped to take a breather about halfway. It was then that I noticed the slight sway of the structure, not a sensation experienced in mountaineering. Clipped on, I relaxed against the hoop at my back. The stink of hydrocarbons drifted past, not unusual in an oil processing works and yet I expected something sweeter at this height.

Time to move on; so I unclipped and climbed once more into even more hydrocarbons the higher I progressed. Clip, unclip, climb four more rungs, lean on hoop, clip-on again; and so it continued.

At last, the top was there and with little effort, Galloway's device was bolted in place and the power wire's end dropped to my boss below. The sway on the structure was quite marked with a frequency of around five seconds. That and the reek of the chemicals lulled me into a state of drowsiness hard to fight. My eyes closed. I lost any sense of my situation. I slumped and slept with my body looped backwards over the top hoop straining against my clipped safety line. Hallucinations invaded my mind. I call them hallucinations for want of an alternative.

Visions of past friends floated before me and were gone in a puff. Grotesque shapes in forbidding colours streamed in front of me, crimson mingled with amber and emerald, traffic lights of the mind. They gushed through my vision, all the time changing shape and suggesting another world of weird and unearthly beings. Darker blobs with surreal eyes hypnotised my mind, floating past on an ever-flowing sea of colour, of vermillion speckled with gold and dripping with viridescent greens. Horror filled my thoughts and I fancy I screamed. A soothing hand caressed my brow and I was aware of falling into a deep, dreamless sleep.

Awareness returned with a hospital odour and I opened my eyes. A voice declared, "I see you are back with us at last."

I could just make out a hazy image of a nurse hovering by my bed. "What happened? Did I fall?" I asked.

The nurse seemed to have the whole story, by her way of it. "It seems you passed out at the top of that ladder. Some steeplejacks on site set up a sling and lowered you to safety. Then you were brought here. That was two days ago." She left it at that.

Later, a doctor filled in some of the spaces. "The gases lingering around the top of that chimney seem to have got to you. I don't know if you realise that hydrocarbons, in particular ethylene, are hallucinogenic. That's what's been causing all the screams and tantrums over the past couple of days. We thought you were on some drug or other and I suppose you were. Anyway, it's out of your system now and you should be up and about later today."

That afternoon, Galloway visited me in the ward. He greeted me friendly enough but I must confess that I was wary and in turn reserved my enthusiasm. We talked about this and that and eventually got round to the 'incident' on the chimney.

He broached the subject carefully. "We really panicked when you started screaming and waving your legs and arms about particularly as you were balanced on that hoop. I don't know why you didn't fall."

"Disappointed, were you?"

"Oh! Don't be like that, Kenny. We were very concerned." He seemed embarrassed by my attitude. "Tommy Henderson brought you down in a cradle. Apparently that's what you should have been wearing in the first place."

"Thank Tommy, will you."

"Sure, sure. We are going to test the ignition system next Thursday. Do you think you'll be fit enough to come along?" Galloway asked and he added as an additional incentive, "The work's manager is going to be there." So what!

That evening, I left for home and another long sleep without any strange nightmares.

Thursday arrived. I made a point of attending the grand opening and joined the small group gathered around the test stack. After the greetings and all the concerned "How are you – alright? – good to see you," and so on, the flame lighting tests began.

First the gas to the pilot line was opened, the switch pressed and a slight pop indicated that the small flame had lit. We all focused on the top of the stack with various binoculars brought along for the event. Now to try the main flame. It too lit and roared away ruling out any words of congratulation. I could plainly see the pilot light in the glare of the flare. I did notice that the pilot tube really was too high and extended into the flare; indeed it was just above the flare's cone, its hottest part.

I watched transfixed as the pilot tube started to melt and bent further and further over. The roar of the flare cut out any warning as the brass tube broke away, fell, bounced once on the ladder, fell further and straight into James Galloway's forehead. He staggered around for some moments like a wounded unicorn, then dropped to the ground.

Galloway lived but they found later that many of his motor faculties had gone and alas, he was confined to a specialist hospital for the rest of his days.

As for me, I left that company. Can you blame me! I still

get hallucinations occasionally, the garish colours, in particular various reds, mascara shaded blobs but with the periodic addition of a shape something like a unicorn. I think I'm finished with chemistry.

THE COTTAGE AT THE END OF THE LANE

We had just moved into our house in the village. It was a modern house – well, modern for those days – red brick construction, red pantile roof, red virgin soil garden and all surrounded by a red wall. The neighbour's house was similar as were a hundred others round about. Every working day, I walked down the lane to the main road where I caught the local bus for my half-hour journey to my new job. As ever, the service was erratic and we commuters spent many a wait at the bus stop exchanging a greeting or two if the sun deigned to appear, or a grunt or two if it were inclement.

At the corner opposite, there stood the quaintest of cottages in brown-stone. It must have been there since some bygone age, for the grey slate roof sagged alarmingly as the years caught up. What was most striking, however, were the touches of brilliant green, intense enough to cheer up the most dismal of days; green window frames, green shutters, green door, green soffits and green gables. Even the garden gate was green. The only concession was the red ceramic chimney pot.

The garden of the cottage glowed in its autumn colours,

amber, marigold and purple; but this wilted as the year moved into autumn and darkness invaded. All too soon, we were into winter and my walk down the lane stumbled into a hike around obstacles of a dimly lit foot slog. At the end of the lane, the cottage passed into mourning in the sodium yellow of the street lighting. Its black shutters became eye patches and soffits were black armbands grieving for a lost summer. Waiting at the bus stop facing the bleak Yorkshire winds with occasional drizzle sometimes spiced with hail, became something of an ordeal. I longed for the day when I could afford a car.

All this passed and we were into spring. The cottage garden came to life with mainly yellows merging later to the various pinks of blossom The rising heat of summer produced a picture book of colour complete with implausible hollyhocks and lupins and various patches of scarlet, white and blue. Even the roses appeared more opulent swanking in their neat, weed-free borders. And the strange thing was that I never ever saw anyone tending all these plants.

One evening I hurried home full of enthusiasm. "Kate," I said, "have you seen the garden down the lane, you know, the one at the cottage?" The blank look was answer enough. She had not seen it. "Tomorrow's Saturday. We'll go down that way for our shopping."

Saturday came, a clear summer's day and off we set on our mission with my zeal and Kate's confusion. I gabbled continuously about flowers and colour and old-worldliness and pretty cottages. Then all was bewilderment for there at the end of the lane there was no cottage, no cottage garden, no anything; only a derelict plot of land, some rubble and a broken chimney pot

… a red chimney pot. Embarrassed I went off with Kate to help with the shopping.

Thoughts of the cottage bothered me. The illusion was so real with all its vivid colours and its changes with the seasons. I just couldn't accept that it was all in the mind.

After several restless nights with peculiar fantasies of fairies and garden gnomes running around weeding this and fixing that, I decided that enough was enough. I had to find out more about that derelict site. I would start with local authority building plans, something I was familiar with when searching for information on our own house.

Searching through the local authority archives, I found the plot for the end of the lane and right enough, there was a cottage on the site, date uncertain. It had the enigmatic title, *Overset* and probably dated back to the 18th century, although even that was uncertain. The whole affair was turning into a mystery for there was no indication of ownership, neither for the original property, the current owner nor anyone in between.

It was difficult to determine where I should turn to next although no doubt there would be County archives and failing that, the National archives. Being of a sensitive nature, I did not wish to appear daft chasing some figment of my imagination. I'll ask Harry Bottom, the local builder of my house. I had spoken to him a few times and found him quite approachable.

That afternoon I spoke to Harry in his office under the clock tower and inquired about the little cottage, indeed about the mysterious wilderness of a plot that remained. "Oh, I know the land you're talking about," said Harry. "I've been after that for ages but I've yet to find an owner. I've passed it over to my solicitor but he hasn't found any trace of the holder as yet."

"What about the original building; anything there?" I pursued.

"There was something there but that was before my time. Hold on. I have the ground plans here;" and with that he went rummaging through a very wide chest of drawers, obviously designed for such plans.

After some time, he extracted a rather dusty map of the corner site of the lane and spread it on his table. It looked just like the one in the local archives and was probably a copy. We huddled over the sheet for some time searching for some enlightenment yet it still failed to divulge anything significant. There was something that I hadn't before noticed essentially because it was not within the plot. "What is that little square there on the opposite side of the cross-road? There seems to be something written there, *Mg132,* I think."

Harry produced a magnifier and his ruler. "You're quite right. I think it's a meter of some sort. Yes! The size is just about right. It'll be a little brick building about a metre square with a concrete top. You see them all over. They have a little door for security – no windows." We left it at that.

On my way home, I again passed the cottage site at the end of the lane; and right enough, there was the little meter block-house on the diagonally opposite corner. Out of curiosity, I crossed over to have a closer look. The meter house was as Harry had described, about a metre square, a metre high, a concrete top, no windows and that solitary door. It looked ancient with tarred wood, rusty hinges and a primitive lock which was no lock at all;

merely a swivel which could be operated with a square-section turn key, the type railway guards used to unlock carriage doors.

I returned home full of resolve. When I had some time to spare, I would return with a suitable turn-key and a torch. I hoped to find some clue within the meter house regarding its age and any labels with ownership, or perhaps the name of the water supplier or even the name of the house across the way.

Come the weekend, I again took myself to the meter house armed with a square section turnkey and a torch. There, I unlocked the door and managed to open it with some difficulty and creaking of rusty hinges, but only after I realised that the door opened outwards. Inside, sure enough, a dusty meter dial stared back. The pipe connecting the device had been isolated on the exit side and chopped through. No one was going to get any free water from this company.

There was no indication of the identity of the former customer so I started raking around the concrete floor. Perhaps there was a discarded label or indeed something to date or name the owner. There was something in the recess behind the meter. It seemed there was a heavy ring set into the floor and a bit more clearing revealed a trapdoor of sorts. No amount of pulling and puffing would budge the barrier. This called for something heavier; another trip home for something like a crowbar.

Another journey home was rewarded with a tyre lever I didn't know I had. Back then, to a little more larceny on the lone meter house with my attempts to prise back the trap door, alas without success. It was only then that I spotted traces of another lock, again of the square-hole variety. The hole was packed with the dirt and mud of ages and it was some time before I managed to clear out this debris. Inserting the turnkey, the lock turned with ease and I was able to lift the trapdoor without the need of a lever.

I peered down the hole into the depths and with the aid of my torch, I could see quite clearly, a set of stone or concrete steps leading off into the gloom. It was at this point that I hesitated; should I follow this trail into the unknown, trespassing into someone else's space, or should I accept the prudent choice and leave it for another day, perhaps never? Curiosity won.

Gingerly I place one foot on the first step, then another and another. Soon I seemed to be descending into the bowels of the earth. That changed. A crumbling step caught me unawares and propelled me down a slippery section. With my behind acting as a sledge, I completed the remaining section onto the earthen floor. My torch with a mind of its own clattered off to its destiny, smashed and snuffed it. This left me in the dark, but, not quite. There seemed to be a quiet glow with no sense of its source. Before me was a bricked arch leading to a void, to an unknown.

My eyes grew accustomed to this dull senseless cavity and I stepped through the archway. In a blink, all whirled in a meaningless fashion and steadied almost immediately. I rationalised the phenomenon to the stale, almost musty air for there was this almost unearthly suspicion of decay around. I shouldn't have been surprised, for I was someway underground - and getting deeper.

I was conscious of shadows moving around me; yet I was confused, for I could not determine any shape. These shapes hugged the earthy ceiling and seemed to move randomly. In addition, the top was some distance away and my eyesight is not great. Then it came to me in a flash; these were human shapes and they were walking upside down on the roof of the cave.

By the dismal light, I edged closer to one of the sidewalls, really to have something to steady myself and my nerves. Touching the side, I could feel the cold, damp clay and I shivered. Yet something was pulling me to that wall, almost like a magnet and before I realised, I was walking up the wall to the roof. Indeed, I became one of the ceiling walkers. Now, I didn't feel upside down. This was my new *terra firma.*

The shadowy figures around me became real people though they still ignored me and I did wonder if they could see me at all. The gloomy light showed up everyday items, trees, stone walls, wooden fences, but the light, having no single source, cast no shadows. The result was the eye perceiving all in two dimensions, a flat comic book picture.

I wandered around this unreal flat world unable to accept its reality. There was the occasional cottage surrounded by its own little garden, some with flowers, others vegetables. Inevitably, I recognised the cottage with the green shutters, a rather dull green because of the beggarly light. Pausing before the green gate, I debated whether to knock and make myself known, for, of course they were strangers. I almost felt like Frankie Vaughan and his *Green Door* number. (Gosh! That takes me back!) Again, curiosity won and I knocked, waited and knocked again. The door slowly opened of its own accord; I guess it hadn't been latched properly – perhaps. Poking my nose in, I found what I think was some sort of vestibule with a wooden partition and another green door. Emboldened, I pushed open this door and stepped into a vast long hall. I was aware of a jumble of numerous voices all talking across each other. Their echoes bounced back from lofty rafters in great surges of sound like the waves of the ocean. This was a giant conch shell full of the surf of voices from bass to treble.

From this bombora stepped the figure of a jolly woman, round faced with a perpetual smile. She greeted me with, "Step in, step in, sir! Don't let the sound of these vain voices intimidate you."

I hesitated. "I … I don't want to interrupt the meeting …"

The woman continued to beckon and gestured at the assembly, almost with contempt. "They just sit at this table all day, talking, talking, talking about everything – except Death. They continually talk and stare straight ahead at nothing – and hear nothing; for they don't listen to each other. And all the time they tremble as though expecting some happening. The only time they look at each other is when Death sweeps past. They then look briefly and return to their pointless talking. With keys jangling on his belt and a long pen behind an ear, Death carries two passports, one marked Heaven the other Hell. He passes on,"

"This is Purgatory, then," I asked?

"You could call it that," she replied and smiled wickedly. "But don't just stand there, Laddie. Come on in!"

I'd heard enough. I backed through the inner door, quickly through the vestibule and out to join the shadowy figures, if that's what they were. I prefer to think of them as shades waiting to take their places at the long table, the table of perpetual voices. Running at full tilt, I made off in any direction as long as it was away from the Green House. Here and there I searched for the brick archway, the only landmark known to me. To no avail! Panic!

I sat on a stone dyke to catch my breath and also to collect my thoughts. "*The Green House is over there, I think.*" It was only a wild guess but I had to start somewhere. "*The arch should be over there – perhaps. Or over there?*" In the panic, I hadn't realised that I was searching for the wrong thing. I should be looking for a V-shape, the arch inverted. And there it was over to my right.

I quickly slithered down the clay wall to regain my own dimension. There through the archway was the crumbling concrete stairway to the upper world, my world. Up and through the trapdoor into the meter house and out into the dusk of an evening, I fled.

Slowly, I made my way up the lane and home to be greeted by, "Where have you been? Tea was half an hour since. What a mess! Straight into the bath for you." Me? I just try not to remember the brink of Hell I'm trying to forget.

SATISFACTION

Gone are the days when adverts were optional. They appeared on billboards, in newspapers or on any old walls. You either looked at them or really didn't notice. Things have changed. Advertising is essentially confined to TV and you can't really avoid it. Even BBC has its own sneaky adverts probably some trailer for a programme to appear at some date in the distant future.

You are sitting there in your favourite armchair munching an apple and drinking in the latest Western when up on the screen there is an advert for something you can't do without. The controllers of such things are really crafty, for they push these adverts into the middle of the most exciting parts. Then again, they seldom place an advert at the beginning of a programme; they wait until you are hooked, then plonk - in goes the advert.

Being of an age when I have a little leisure time – that is, I'm retired – I tend to watch Tele on afternoons. Many older-generation folk are the same. As a consequence, the adverts are geared towards us. They fall into two categories: Death and Money. It's time to plan for your funeral with this wonderful insurance plan; or maybe leave cash to your "loved ones." Do you know how much it costs these days? Etc. etc.

As for the money adverts, they are again some kind of insurance system. These try to entice you to release the equity of your house so that you can spend it, or give it away to those "loved ones" or the ideal holiday you've always longed for. In other words, put your house in hock for some extra spondulicks.

Such adverts play on the emotions, try to make you feel guilty. They point out that there are others in the family who are a bit short of the readies and that you have the potential to provide the moolah. Well, so be it and that is up to the individual. They don't bother me particularly. What I really hate are those insurance ones which use babies faces and edit their mouth movements to mime adult voices – shudder. I'm sure it qualifies as child labour.

The problem for me is that I believe what I read and see in adverts. The result is that I have put down payments on something like five coffins and paid for them with the equity release on my home.

One advert in the local paper did catch my eye, however, for it was related to one of my many interests. Brief and to the point, it ran like this:

Temporary Post
Aide required to assist in project
On the Nature and Origin
Of Symbolism.
Small stipend offered to suitable candidate.
(Apply to Box 1342 by 12th April)

Out of interest, I sent in an application listing past experience in ESP testing and fraudulent detection and duly received a reply asking me to attend an interview at The Victoria Hotel in West River Street on 17th April.

On that day of the 17th, I donned my best tweeds and duly arrived at the Victoria Hotel on the appointed hour. I was directed to room 209 on the second floor and thence, via a notice, to a 'comfortable' Victorian room with a scattering of very upright chairs and an equally hard chaise longue in black bombazine. Seated at an ancient oak desk was an equally ancient time-worn gentleman all prepared to find out my background and expertize in the realms of symbolism.

"Come in! Come in and sit down!" he said. "I have your letter with details, such as they are. I am Jules Corelli – perhaps you have heard of me - and I am conducting this piece of research starting with some work on ESP." He frowned at me across his rimless spectacles and rubbed his chin vigorously with a sandpaper sound. "Later, I hope to extend this to symbols of various types." He frowned again. His conversation was a sort of meandering between the weather and symbols exploration; indeed, I found it difficult to follow his train of thought blended with a trace of madness.

After a bit, he exclaimed, "You don't seem to have done much along these lines." What did he mean! I hadn't said a word during this jumble and I came to the conclusion that he himself had done little interviewing in his past. "Why do you think you would be suitable for this job?"

"Well, Mr Corelli, I don't know what the job involves. The advert didn't say much and you haven't said a lot about the nature of the research; so I don't know if my experience would relevant."

"Oh dear, oh dearie me," was his response and he rubbed his chin again and stared at me through his lenses.

"If it's about ESP testing, I could be useful in identifying people who are trying to cheat. You see, I have quite an extensive knowledge of this through my time as a professional magician."

He nodded in approval and rubbed his chin. "I know, I know," he said. "Ideal for this. I think I can offer you the job."

I sat back astonished, for I had gone through many job interviews in my past and had never been offered one on the spot. "Oh yes. I think I can offer you the post of research assistant to the project director – that's me. You see, you are the only applicant." A compliment, indeed!

Is this an April fool's prank, rather an elaborate one? I thought.

* * *

I started my part-time low-paid job the following Monday. The 'office' was a little room, part of Mr Corelli's home. We both sat at a little round Elmwood table with blank pads of paper before us. It was apparent that we were starting at square one, which made me wonder why we were starting at all. Had he done any research into extra sensory perception or was this just one of his whims?

"So; where do we start, Mr Corelli and what are we trying to do?"

"Just call me Jules and I'll call you Ken. My curiosity was

aroused by an experiment I was involved in last year. It was to do with standard ESP cards, you know the sort of thing. The two participants sit in their own little cubical; one stares at a card picked at random and the other scribbles on a pad any shape that comes to mind. Of course, the recipient knows the five shapes he is limited to and so has a one in five odds of being correct. Even so, I seemed to be about 80% correct."

I recognised the pattern of the tests. I also recognised the basis for cheating depending on the pattern of the choice method. It is the basis for several conjuring tricks, sometimes with a sixth symbol, namely a triangle, so that the system can also be used with a dice. I don't know why a hexagon is not used to keep it in line with numbers for each symbol. I explained this to Jules for he seemed unaware of this connection.

"It's like this, Jules. The number one is associated with a circle as this symbol uses one line; two with two lines of a cross; three with three wavy lines; four with the four sides of a square; five with the five points of a star. It's a useful association in tricks but if there is any hint of this in any ESP test, you begin to smell a rat."

I then showed this using a couple of simple tricks. It all looked like genuine ESP but I assured him that it was all trickery without revealing the method. I would have been drummed out of the Magic Circle if I had divulged that. Having convinced him that such skulduggery exists, we got on with the serious matter of genuine telepathy.

Jules would set up various situations for tests with five ESP cards and I would try to devise some sort of deception around his restrictions. It was very much like the restrictions

Harry Houdini would place on his escapology tricks. However, I drew the line at being handcuffed, chained up, blindfolded and lowered headfirst into a tank of water. On one occasion, though, I allowed a blindfold though I took care to seat myself strategically in line with a convenient mirror. Mind you, the restrictions he devised were not all that sophisticated.

We played with various ideas over the next few weeks. I felt though, that Jules was getting bored with all my debunking of his 'fool-proof' experiments. In a way he wanted to believe that thought transference was possible and in a way it is. It is just that silly little artificial setups, where the mind was forced to jump, just did not work. The process had to be spontaneous and I think he accepted this conclusion. Perhaps our study could take a different direction, a tangent to our present one though I had the feeling that Jules was becoming exasperated with my conjuring tricks.

A couple of desultory weeks later, Jules let me into the office. There was a decided spring to his step and he could hardly wait to tell me all about it, whatever that 'it' was. "Sit down, Kenny, sit down! Let me tell you about an idea I have," he declared almost bubbling over in his excitement. "Do you know of a place called Machrihanish?" He noted my blank look and continued; "It's a wee place at the west end of The Mull of Kintyre. I've booked us into a hotel there for Thursday of this week, just for a few days." I still looked blank.

"May I ask why?" I thought I'd better ask; and what had this to do with ESP; or was this a completely different tack, another madcap idea? Indeed he had a suggestion of slyness in his manner.

"Well, it's like this," he continued. "There is this wifey who lives there, a Meg Campbell. I was reading this article about mysterious thought transference experiences and they mentioned this Meg Campbell who apparently has second sight."

I sighed. "Do you know what second sight is?"

He looked slightly embarrassed and hesitated.

I continued, "It is something in Gaelic culture and is interpreted as someone with two sights; one sees the living, the other the dead. Sometimes it means someone who can see the present with one sight and the future with the other. So this Meg has the second sight, has she?"

"Yes, that'll be right." He seemed a bit uncertain and annoyed, but let it go at that. "I thought she might have a different slant on ESP – we could follow up." Jules still seemed unsure and troubled.

That was it. We were off on the long road to Machrihanish – and Jules would be driving.

* * *

Come Thursday and we took off in Jules's Mini with him driving as planned. Did I say that Jules was driving? I suppose that you could call it that; still, I think I'll drive in future if I have a choice in the matter. The problem was that when talking he would look face-on at his companion – and he talked a lot. Meantime I stared ahead at an uncertain future that only Meg could foretell. Some Highland roads twist in an uncertain fashion.

Arriving at Inveraray, we parked the car at the harbour and

had lunch at a little hotel there. "Would you like me to take over the driving?" I asked, recalling the twisted road before us. He refused. His car insurance covered only himself as driver, so I had no way out there.

Off we continued down Loch Fine. There was nothing for it but to grit my teeth and think of the hereafter. The road was better than I remembered and soon we were through Lochgilphead and on to Tarbert. The road took us west to the Atlantic side of the Mull with sight of the Isles of Jura and Islay. Further as dusk was setting in, we could see the Island of Gigha and a little further the road forked right for Machrihanish, a scattering of a few houses with our hotel overlooking a golf course. I gratefully prised myself from the sweaty plastic seat, opened the car door and thankfully sniffed the salty air and the future.

Over the evening meal in our hotel, we discussed our approach to our second sight subject. Should we just march up to the lady's door or is there another more subtle approach. First we must find where she lives.

"I say," Jules approached our serving waitress, "could you tell us where Meg Campbell lives?" Ah yes, the subtle approach.

She looked at us quizzically. "Oh aye, Old Meg. She's in that wee cottage at the end of the village. You can't miss it. It's the house with the tin roof, but dinna go there in the dark. It's best to keep clear when it's dark," she added ominously.

Jules nodded his thanks and turned to me with a mystified look. Things are looking curiouser and curiouser.

That night in the chill of my bedroom, I felt a certain apprehension about the whole project. How can you march up to a stranger's door and exclaim, "What do you know about ESP?" And the window replied with a distinctly rattled, "Daft". This conversation with a chatting window continued long into the night.

Next morning, suitably replenished with porridge and well happed up against the Atlantic chill, we strode briskly along the village's only street in the direction of the cottage. There was no mistaking it with its rusty corrugated iron roof. It was a sandstone property, ancient but not rundown. To the lee side there appeared to be a herb garden sheltered from the snell winds by a copse of pines.

As we strode up the gravel path, the cottage door opened and Meg appeared, a plaid shawl in bright colours protected her shoulders and reflected in her rimless spectacles. "I've been expecting you," she said (so she did have the second sight after all). "Have you come to have your fortune told, then?" and I thought I could detect a caustic glint in her eye. "Peggie at the hotel said you were asking after me." (No second sight there, then!)

"No, no," Jules said taking the bait. Yet, I had that uneasy feeling that the two had met before. I don't know why. It was just one of those feelings. Yet two disparate characters I have still to find. He went on to introduce us and explain our mission, our ESP experiments and our future plans.

"Don't just stand there, laddies. Come in and I'll make us all a cup of tea," she commanded. I thought; she called me a laddie – such flattery. It's a long time since I was called that. "What kind would you prefer? I can offer you peppermint, nettle or camomile."

We both went for the camomile and I'll bet she made her own deductions from our choice – very clever, these soothsayers.

I promptly felt uneasy as I entered the cottage. I immediately knew I was in the presence of … what? … a *familiar* perhaps? Yes! It was a cat and I am allergic to cats. There it was lurking in the shadows. I could barely see its black shape and its not so glowing amber eyes and a passage came to mind:

Hold back the talons of your paws,
Let me gaze into your beautiful eyes of metal and agate.

My own eyes fired up and itched abominably with tears of allergy running and nose stinging. I apologised, and left Jules to Meg's company with a brief explanation of my hay fever.

After five minutes in the cold wind, I made my way back to the hotel for a cheerless cup of tea and waited. After some time, Jules returned full of ideas and information that I found difficult to untangle but eventually gathered. It concerned a cave on some local island with mysterious signs. It was Davaar Island.

"If we stay here overnight, we can explore the island tomorrow," Jules suggested. "It's just over the other side of Campbeltown," he continued with just too much enthusiasm for my liking.

"What did Meg put in your camomile tea back there?" but let it go at that.

Next day, we went off to Campbeltown to find out more about this island. Apparently, you can walk over to Davaar Island at low tide and the causeway was passable for about 4 hours; so we would have plenty of time for our exploration.

It is not all that easy or comfortable walking over a pebble beach. We reached the island and paused. We should have brought some sandwiches, I thought, yet struggled on to these secret caves. Indeed, they were so secret, there was a notice declaring TO THE CAVES in giant letters. I did wonder about continuing even so as we continued our walk over close cropped grass and finally more loose pebbles.

There at last was the cave, just before us. Now I should declare that another of my phobias is enclosed spaces and in particular caves. My hair bristles and I feel the presence of 'things unknown', spooky things, perhaps supernatural things. This cave was no different. I went cold all over and started to tremble. This was not helped when further into the cave we came across a picture of the Crucifixion painted on the raw rock. That was all I needed and I exited in double quick time.

I was still there when Jules came out some time later. He was all excited and declared he had found some signs further in, runes he called them. His eyes, bright and shiny bore into me with a sort of mania, almost as though some kind of drug careered through his veins, a hallucinogen perhaps. With great reluctance I ventured further in.

"See! There, there," he cried flashing his torch into an opening at the far end of the cave. "Do you see on the far wall, the carvings, the runes?" Caught up in his enthusiasm, I push in further and peered at the wall seeing nothing and was about to tell him so when the light went out. There was a grating sound followed by a clunk. I was completely enclosed in this dark place. No glimmer of light, just this Stygian black of a tomb – which it was.

Immediately, panic set in as I fumbled around the walls of my prison shouting all the while, screaming till I was hoarse. No reply. No sign. In the silence, the graveness of my situation grew. The realisation hit me that the whole *search for signs* thing was a ploy to lure me to this place. But why?

My claustrophobia vanished and anger took over. Shouting brought no response and I doubted whether there would be any other visitors this late in the holiday season. I sat there fuming at my circumstances and took stock of my resources. I searched through the pockets of my anorak: a pencil, pen, a navigation compass from my sailing days, a rope knife with blade and marlin spike – all useful things in the right situation but useless in the dark. Then there was my mobile phone. Of course! I fumbled around and manage to switch it on. There was no signal in the middle of my rocky tomb, but at least I now had some light from its torch App.

The light from the torch showed solid rock walls all around my crypt. I was so disorientated that I couldn't find the location of the original doorway. There was barely enough room to stand upright as my head touched the gravelly ceiling. No magic opening, no break in the rock face, no sliding panels. I was doomed to this freezing, damp hell-hole.

I sat on a wet stone thinking in the dark. There must be some solution, surely. I must not give up. Glancing round my dark prison I imagined that it wasn't quite black. Light seemed to be seeping in somewhere. Yes! There along a little was a gem reflected from a rock with its source somewhere overhead. Of course! The roof was gravel. I felt it with my head when I first stood and if light managed to get through, so could I.

The marlin spike of my knife was the ideal digging tool and I started picking at the roof. The roof loosened and showered gravel all around with a gap appearing overhead. A little more effort and the hole was large enough for me to haul myself through. I lay there panting with my efforts and gratefully drew in the evening air.

As I looked around, I could see that the tide had risen and was already lapping at the cave entrance. That meant that the causeway would be covered and there was no way off the island. Better look for shelter, I thought. It would be dark come the next low tide. Walking round the headland I noticed that the causeway was indeed covered. There in the gloaming I could see the lighthouse, just a glimmer of white but enough to guide me there. There would be no one there for they are all unmanned these days but its walls would provide some shelter from the evening breeze. The door to the keeper's cottage might even be unlocked.

The last of the day had disappeared by the time I reached the cottage, the locked cottage. However, there was a lock-safe next to the door and that was no barrier to an ex-assistant to the Great Dante, the magician. It was a safe which required a four number code plus a letter, five minutes to open when you know how. Inside was a sitting room, a bedroom and a shower room plus toilet and the whole place was electrically heated, fine and cosy. My guess is that it was used as a holiday cottage in season. A quick shower and a stretch out on the couch. If I didn't use the bed and left everything neat and tidy, no-one would know I had been. There was tea for a quick brew but the fridge only revealed some out-of-date yogurt.

As I lay there on the couch, I planned my next move. First I must get back to home soil where all my resources lay; then I would devise some sort of retribution. After all, I don't take kindly to being killed – even though it was unsuccessful.

After a fitful night and a fiendish plan in my head, I could see that the causeway was open. I crossed quickly to the Mull of Kintyre mainland, entered the nearest café and ordered a bacon saney and coffee for breakfast. A few enquiries and I later boarded the bus for Glasgow arriving some five hours later. Now to set about my plan.

As you know, I have a long and varied experience in the world of magic, the conjuring type. Firstly, I had to develop a method for producing a 'ghost' of myself; easy enough to do in a theatre environment. It was an effect I had worked on some years previously, to produce an image in any situation. I used the 'Pepper's Ghost' method but using lasers and electrical fields instead of spotlights and mirrors. It worked well enough with a little imagination and certainly well enough to fool Jules in his present state. I would scare him out of his wits. I prepared a recording of my voice with a few key phrases and added an echo over the voice. To add to the special effects, I devised a radio-controlled solenoid to attach to his door knocker and a similar device for his electric door bell. Thus, I was all ready with my nefarious plan.

It was late autumn and dark nights had come. I went to the street where Jules lived. I had photographed it many times with my mobile phone. The laser guns would be placed there, there and there. I had already disconnected the street light nearest his house to give a reasonable pool of darkness. The gaffed knocker and doorbell were in place - so the stage was set. In the gloom, I could see that his car was parked near his entrance and a chink of light from the drawn curtains all showed that he was at home. Time to begin.

In the anonymous darkness of my distant parked car, I rang his doorbell with my device. The hall light glowed, the door opened, a head poked out and looked both ways. Yes! It was Jules. I picked up my mobile, the throw away type, and rang his number. After some time, he answered: "Yes?"

I ran the first recorded message. In a turgid, doom laden voice (complete with echo) it said, "I'm so cold, so cold … " He slammed down the receiver. I left a gap before I tried again. He lifted the phone but said nothing.

In the same grim voice and a touch of desperation, "Get me out Jules!" Then a groan. The phone went down.

I'll try the door knocker, two ponderous bang … bangs. Tentatively, the door open and Jules ventured a timid look around. That was when I switched on the laser show with an image of me drifting past. That was enough. The door slammed and I could hear a bolt being slammed into place.

With my show finished, I collected my bits and pieces and drove home, my first part completed.

Next day, I drove along the street of last night's escapade to judge the reaction, if any. I was not disappointed. Jules's car had gone, either to Mystic Meg's (for another consultation) or to Davaar Island to see whether I was still there – or rather, my body. It had been two weeks since my supposed entombment so by rights I should be dead by now.

I determined to follow to Machrihanish and judge for

myself. I loaded my car with a few essentials, biscuits, drinks, the disposable mobile, walking boots and binoculars; a quick check on the petrol situation and off now to observe the two culprits.

Arriving at Machrihanish, I parked at the golf course lost among the other cars there and fished out the binos. Yes! There it was. Jules's car was blatantly parked at Meg's cottage, so I was right. The two of them were in this together. I sat there with binos handy expecting a long wait and nibbled biscuits.

It was a long wait.

I got to thinking that if those two come out, go to Jules's car and drive off, they are going to notice me following with so little traffic around. I decided, therefore, to forestall them and anticipated that they would go back to Davaar Island to confirm my demise – or otherwise. Off I went to the car park near the island at Campbeltown. I didn't stop there for my lone car would be just too obvious. Instead, I drove down a side track out of sight yet with the island still in view. The causeway was just starting to uncover with the falling tide. Perhaps they had been waiting for that.

Right on cue, I could hear their car approaching and then the two doors slamming shut. There they were, striding across the shingle and onto the island. To my surprise, they didn't follow the coast to the caves but took a shortcut across the tufted grass with Meg leading the way. I took some pictures of the two striding away with the distance between them growing. Nearing their destination, Jules suddenly disappeared. He had accidently found my escape hole; he was there one minute, the next he was gone - like some staged illusion. As I watched through my binoculars, Meg looked back and saw nothing. I could plainly see her shocked expression, then fear. Perhaps she did believe in goblins and kelpies.

Quickly she left the island, crossed the causeway and returned to the car. It was locked. She scurried back to Campbeltown and disappeared from sight.

Thinking about the situation, I decided to execute the final phase. After all, I couldn't just leave Jules stuck down a hole in the middle of nowhere. I picked up the throwaway mobile and called the police. Disguising my voice (I trust) I outlined the story, just twisted somewhat; "I've just seen Meg Campbell push a man down a hole on Davaar Island."

Police, "Where, Sir?"

"Davaar Island near Campbeltown. I think the man was Jules Corelli."

I tossed that phone into the sea and left events to take their course.

A SACRED PLACE

As I LOOK OUT TO the sea-scape beyond the dunes of sand and rough, sharp grass, I realise that I have made it at last. I have retired. "About time too!" declare many who have watered and fed me over the years. And why not? I have listen to their problems and solved some of them and, at times, have created new ones. They may be correct but it is a bit hard that they say I am the problem.

Anyway, here I am retired. I have my little cottage, quite small yet it does me fine. I have a great view over the ever-changing sea and from my kitchen, the hills roll away to the eastern horizon with patches of woodland here and there. The cottage should be cosy enough with its triple glazing, but when the Westerlies come chapping, they seem to find every little gap in the structure. Outside there is a small garden of sorts with little surviving in the sand. The path to the porch is guarded by two small trees: a hawthorn – all angles and elbows – and a rowan – all grace and elegance. I call them Gog and Magog, hoping that they will grow taller. A dirt track leads to my nearest neighbour, Dougie, about two miles south and continues beyond to so-called civilization.

I have spent a lifetime searching out the unexplained and the mysterious, a sort of hobby you might say. However, that was not my daytime job. Then, I was a teacher of chemistry; perhaps you have seen my book on chemistry problems. That is all behind me now and I have retired to the uncomplicated remoteness of the countryside and to while away my remaining time thinking of the simplicity of this bucolic life – and wallow in it.

For a time all was well. If it were wet outside, I would sit in and read a book or ponder over past adventures, an expression for falling asleep in my comfortable armchair. Whiles on a good day, I would wander a staggering path over grass tussocks to the edge of the sea. I would even dip my toes in the icy water, just to frighten the fish. More often than not though, I would simply skirt the water and seat myself on a convenient rock to listen to the waves playing with the white shell sand. I was on the edge of boredom.

Come spring and the machair bloomed with its brilliantly coloured jewels - orchids, bluebells, long stemmed daisies and a host of others; and with them came their various fragrances to lift the spirits. My boredom vanished.

Some days, the hills would beckon. It was easier following the sheep tracks up and over and past small tree plantations. With the increase in altitude, I could look back at an increased expanse of sea towards some distant islands, mere blue lines on the horizon. I sigh.

Occasional nights when it was clear overhead, I would sit outside and gaze at the stars, the Milky Way sprinkled across the heavens from one horizon to the other, or the Twelve Signs, or just gaze. These were all mysteries beyond my ken.

When out walking the hills, I noticed that there was one stand of trees that was different. These were no Sitka spruce planted for profit. I think they were Scots pines but I could be wrong. They sat on the top of a small rise all alone. The lower limbs had been lopped off to offer a top-heavy look and there was no discernable ground pattern to their planting. With my usual curiosity, I approached the group.

Entering the grove, I could sense an inexplicable atmosphere of calm. The spaced-out trees seemed to present a barrier to outside sounds though I could still hear the lofty tops brushing the breeze but only distantly. I would have expected rooks nesting up there for it was ideally suitable, remote and safe; yet not a sign. It was a sacred place. If anything, it seemed cold even on a warm day like this. For all that, it was a favourite destination for my frequent walks. I looked forward to walking up the incline with this Parthenon in my sights. Within, it was always chilly but with clear uninterrupted views all round.

On one occasion when Dougie visited me and we were sharing some interesting malt, I had the opportunity to ask him about this temple on the hillock.

"Och, that's *Banrigh Reothadh* Woods" he offered tentatively. "We are not after talking about them but they say they are haunted," he continued, but would offer nothing more notwithstanding a further dram or two. Haunted indeed! And who am I to believe that. After all, I was a purveyor of mysteries at one time.

I pursued the subject further. "Who owns the woods then, Dougie?" I asked and looked at him expectantly.

Dougie thought for a moment and answered modestly, "I

suppose I do. This is all my land round here except for the Sitka plantations. *Banrigh Reothadh* Woods have always been there. They've always just looked the same."

I digested all this and left it at that.

The seasons slipped by. Gog displayed an abundance of haws, still green, and Magog a harvest of yellow rowan berries turning orange, all offered to a variety of snooty birds, really after protein for their young. I continued with my walks and observations of the wonders of nature. The changing moods of the sea drew me there more often than not although I did wonder what the winter storms would bring. However, my favourite rest for contemplation was within the mysterious wood on the mound.

I spent many an hour sitting on a rubble of stones in the middle of the temple with my mind drifting to another world where all the woes had been put to rights. The soothing whispering in the pine tops lulled the senses to accept such an impossible state of affairs. One can but dream. Jerking myself away from this Utopia, I would gaze at the sea or turn on my rock to the hills and the mountains beyond. "It's not so bad here really," I thought.

The year continued to drift by, the berries on G and MaG disappeared and the days grew shorter. Before long, it was autumn with leaves everywhere and Magog stood naked by the path while Gog shook his twisted branches with laughter. We moved into November.

I woke one calm morning to whiteness and for a moment I thought the first snow had arrived, but a chaste sea breeze chased the frost away. It was the forerunner of more cold days to come with sunshine moments. On one such day, I walked out and up to the Parthenon to enter the clutch of trees. The frost lay even all around and my footprints left no trail, strange and entrancing. What with the sun and the locale, I seemed to go into a trance and my mind wandered every which way. I was aware of a cold east wind rising. It stirred the frost and the crystals moved among the grasses and into the temple with a sound I can only describe as a brush over a snare drum. Its hissing rose with a crescendo and swirled around to trace a whirl of white, ululating to some primitive sensual strain. It swayed here and there around the tree pillars and soon I was enveloped in its frigid cloud, the crystals stinging my skin, until I felt I was part of the icy maelstrom. For a moment I felt frozen lips touch mine, then it was gone. The wind dropped. The illusion vanished. I staggered along the slippery slope to my but and ben. The bottle of malt did not endure the night.

Next day late, I sought out my friend, Dougie. My face still tingled and my lips were chapped and all glistened with sun cream, ironically. When Dougie saw me, my florid face and cracked lips, he laughed knowingly. "I can see that the frost has been punishing your tender skin," and he laughed again.

I just scowled. "I fell asleep in the wood, the wood with the Scots pines. I suspect I was bewitched by the place," I joked.

"Och, you would, too," he replied. "That's *Coilltean na Banrigh Reothadh*, the Woods of the Frost Queen," he added darkly.

THE VEGETARIAN

HERE I AM IN MY autumn years, sitting slack in my rocker under the porch. I cast my mind back to all those bygone times, those farming years, when autumn was a time of fulfilment - harvests of golden corn anticipating the keen edge of completion as the farmhand hones his scythe. He would open Four Acre Field before I joined him with my scythe. The lassies would follow, tying the sheaves and stooking them to dry in neat castles of six or eight.

Sometime (usually in the afternoons) there would be a welcome pause when the lady of the house would arrive with a basket of goodies to refresh us workers. Newly baked pancakes and scones liberally decorated with the jam of the day and washed down with tea or sometimes home-made Boston cream. The meal was completed with chunks of sultana cake.

In due time, a cart pulled by Nell the horse would enter the field and dried sheaves would be piled high for their brief trek to the yard for stacking. These sheaves would be threshed later, but not too late, to produce the corn riches for carting off to a grain loft for further drying in the gentle breath of air passing through. Periodically it is tossed by a goon in his bare feet, with a shovel letting air evenly through the oats; and finally it is bagged in hessian ready for the miller.

I would look at this wall of hessian with a deep sigh of fulfilment; for this is the true satisfaction from a year's acquaintance with nature.

It was not always so. For many years, my father, and his father, laboured and tilled the ground to bring it to this healthy state to pass on to me when I was ready. As a youngster I would roam the fields, explore the woods and the hidden places all within domain of the farm. On a hot summer's day, I would lie back in the soft grasses of a hay field and put the World as I knew it, to rights. Everyone would have their own hay field, their own sun and perhaps a stoop of lemonade for those thirsty moments. Does not everyone have a life like this?

Our nearest neighbour was a farm about a mile away to the north and occasionally I would see figures moving around there. My father said it was difficult land there, for it was exceedingly stony with sparse soil. It was only fit for sheep walled in by a long dry-stane dyke. That farm was named Ravens' Acre, I think because of the stand of pines and its birds. The thatched building had few outhouses but I could see a little vegetable garden when I was close enough. Occasionally, Ravens' Acre owner would visit us and swap wool for some straw and winter feeding. He seemed friendly enough but constantly worried with drawn features and eyes that watered. Each time he left us, my father would just shake his head and suck his teeth.

One day down by the dyke, a head popped up from the other side and said, "Hullo! My name's Alec but my mother calls me Sanny. What's yours?" It was a laddie about my age, six years old.

"Oh hullo! Mine is David but I'm usually Davy at home."

So began an unusual friendship and a more unusual episode in my life.

We spent our days together exploring further afield, the wild heath of the local moorland and endless forests of mixed trees; Scottish oak, silver birch with its almost white flakey bark, Scots pine and hazel shrubs with the start of nuts. Sanny knew all their names and sometimes on a warm summer evening, we would sit in a woody glade and he would talk to the trees. This seemed strange at first but I soon accepted the idea and there were times when I thought I could hear the trees replying. These conversations did not enter any deep philosophies or world questions, just plain ordinary talk.

These sessions were private and shared with no-one beyond the two of us and when we grew tired of this, we would visit the local stream to try our hand at guddling for trout, invariably without success. Once Sanny did catch an elver but quickly threw it back; he thought it was a snake.

Sanny knew a lot about birds, their names, what they looked like and where to find their nests. There, we could see the various eggs and on one occasion I suggested that we make a collection of eggs. "What!" He said in horror. "We canna take awa' the baby birds!" And I didn't mention the idea again. All day long we searched the bushes alarming blackbirds and thrushes and I noticed a little robin that was quite aggressive, really annoyed at the disturbance. My friend even showed me some ground nests. "That one there," he pointed, "is the nest of a whaup. They are quite easy to find with the bird fussing around all the time." I looked at the brown-speckled green eggs. "Larks are different," he continued. "Ye canna find them at all; anyway, I canna." We continued like this all day till mealtime.

Sanny did have one characteristic which I found difficult to accept; he smelled. He seemed to have an abundance of wind for some reason. I asked him about it once. He didn't seem at all fazed by the question and said that Auntie Jessie had asked the same. The answer seemingly lay in his diet. The family lived essentially on oats and the vegetables grown in the little garden. His favourites were beans and peas. I nodded sagely, without knowing why.

Autumn came and after harvest, we were both of an age to be sent to the local church school. There we both learned the basic art of survival. Not that all the other children were evil, but there were certain ones who took a delight in tormenting Sanny. The school day was over by mid-day when we were all sent on our merry way home. Not that ours was all that merry for he was taunted all the way along that stony path home. I was determined to stick by him but he didn't really need my support for he was growing to be a tough and brawny laddie.

The Dominie was the Kirk minister, tall and spare in stature and sarcastic of tongue, too ready with the tawse when the mood took him. He leathered the letters and numbers into us unfortunates who were not too interested in such things. We were more into country matters. Early on he latched onto Sanny's odour, or as he called it, "Eau de farmyard." He would call Sanny before the class and quizzed him. "Spiers!" he roared. "What dung heap have you been rolling in? Eh! … Eh! Answer me laddie!" Then the tawse would come out. All the time the others would titter and giggle.

When the school day ended at mid-day a group of the 'scholars' would gather and taunt Sanny and it was not long before he picked up the nickname, Smelly Sawney (they dragged out the latter part of his name):

Smelly Sawney had a coo,
It was black aboot the moo.
Wasna that a bonny coo?
Dance Smelly Sawney.[5]

Inevitably, such taunting led to fisticuffs and Sanny soon learned the art of self-defence. He started with an advantage with his burley build and it was not long before they kept clear of his swinging fists, scratching nails and gnashing teeth. They kept up taunts but at a distance.

It reached the stage where he sought out his fight opponents, usually the bigger lads with the raucous voices. His favourite ploy was to bite their ears; the sight of blood soon had them on their way and as he remarked afterwards, "I'm getting a taste for blood!" After a bit, the jeering went and the mob of kids moved on to other easier targets.

Later as we walked home together he reflected; "Ye ken, Davy, ma faither says you've got tae face up tae they things, an he's richt, ye ken." Inwardly, I nodded sagely; again I didn't know why.

Onward through the winter we plodded to school. The snows came – and still school. We exchanged snowballs, had

5. To the tune of Katie Bairdie.

slides (mainly on our bums) and rubbed snow on the lassies' faces. And before we realised it, spring had arrived and the longer days.

The school day finished at 12.00 releasing us for the remainder of the day. Now that we were bigger, we were able to tackle more tasks around the farms. Sanny's working year really began before mine with the lambing season and being a strong lad, he was able to act as midwife at times. He showed me how to, but I didn't have his pulling power and he laughed at my efforts. To tell the truth, I didn't really have the stomach for it either. Anyway, my own tasks were multiplying.

A few years later, things changed. Sanny's father died, his wife moved in with her sister at Lowermains and Sanny disappeared over the horizon. They said that his father could take no more and just gave up. The price of wool plummeted and lamb had no market. There are times now I look across at Ravens' Acre. The house no longer has a thatch, the stane dyke is in ruins and the ground has run wild. Occasional deer venture in to nibble at the grass or the gone-to-seed garden. There are no peas or beans there now.

I finished my local schooling when I was twelve and my father sent me on to the 'Big School', the Grammar School. There I learned more stuff like geometry and proper English and I think I did pick up a few useful things, but it wasn't obvious. My father saw a bit of sense for once and brought me back to the farm. I had the feeling that he sent me in the first place solely to impress the neighbours.

There came the day when I took over the farm and we grew in prosperity. My reputation for good sense grew too and I was highly regarded in the community to such an extent that I was made Sheriff of the area. It was my duty then to judge minor cases of misdemeanour, usually trivial thieving, poaching and the like. Not that I relished the task for I could recall instances in my past when such 'adventures' were commonplace. I was highly thought of as one of those deep thinkers, when in effect I would merely be dreaming of bygone days.

There were two other Sheriffs in my area who were not quite so lenient and one of their cases came to my attention for good reason. The name of the culprit seemed familiar, Sawney Bean as he was now known, and he had been committed to gaol for 3 months for drunken assault. I thought it only right to visit him in his temporary home and arranged to have access the very next day.

The building was a dismal hovel of stone, steel bars and revolting smell. I took along a plug of tobacco to keep his spirits up and as some token of our friendship of yesterday. He recognised me straight away and greeted me as of old but I managed to steer clear of his embrace.

"My but you're lookin' grand and prosperous, Davy lad."

I could not return the compliment, however, but shook his hand warmly enough. We went on to recall our former days at the Kirk School and the fights and the smell. He laughed unreservedly at the memories. "That's why I changed my name to Bean, Davy." And he laughed again.

"Tell me, Sawney, do you still like your beans as much?" I asked.

He turned quiet and seemed about to clam up but instead came to some sort of decision. "You'll no' tell anyone, Davy but ye mind I used to have those playground fights wi' the others, all the scratching and biting."

I nodded. I remembered it well.

"Well, I got a taste for it," he continued. "There are times when I've eaten human flesh – and enjoyed it. Dinna tell anyone. Dinna tell the Sheriff or I'm done for."

I was shocked and backed away. I did not remain for long after and left the dismal place, thinking all the while. The visions and thoughts conjured up stayed with me long afterwards and dominated my nightmares for months until I managed to push them to the recesses of my brain.

Sometime later, the dark thoughts re-emerged. It happened as I was chatting with some colleagues over a glass of claret one evening. Douglas MacVie was issuing forth on the latest news in from the Sheriff's Office in Carrick. "They caught them somewhere down by Ballantrae near Girvan. They had been hiding in some sea caves there and waylaid travellers on the shore road, robbed them, killed them and ate them, so they say. A band of ruffians and cannibals!"

MacVie turned to me; "Are you going to the execution on Friday, Davy? It's up at Dundee at noon; they'll be hanging their leader, Sawney Bean."

Sawney! Not my friend, not him! I then recalled his prison confession. Was I going to his execution? I thought not.

JEAN BLAINE

When I was a youngster, a long time ago I must say, I would cycle everywhere. Really when I say everywhere, my excursions were rather limited, for we lived in an end-of-the-road village. This meant that every journey had one of two options in common; you either covered the section past the Stavanox (locally pronounced Stabneugh) or you took the road past Jean Blaine's.

The Jean Blaine section was unremarkable apart from the sharp turn at the bridge just past her cottage followed by a steep hill, a very steep climb. For the cyclist, this usually meant a dismount and walk with countless backward apprehensive glances at the cottage. Yet we frequently chose that route for it took us the short distance to the Sands of Gora and the sea.

That summer was glorious with endless sun for our school holidays, trips to the sea and oodles of sandy sandwiches. After the red period, we all turned a healthy tanned glow, all except Ginger McCandlish, he of the red hair and the look of a boiled lobster.

So what was so terrible about Jean Blaine or her cottage? Well, gossip had it that she was a witch and funny/peculiar things happened in her cottage. The rumours just stayed suspended in the air without anything specific to back them up; yet they stuck nevertheless. None of my pals had seen her so there was nothing from that quarter apart from lurid tales which I guess were invented on the spot and some said she once had a man, a soldier claimed by war.

It so happened that I enjoyed cycle trips to the sea, to breathe the salt laden air and watch the hesitating tide. There were times when we would go bathing as a group and chase the tiny fishes that would come nibbling at our toes. The various sea birds would ignore us and just continue with their search for food. All except the gulls who could sniff out a sandwich from a mile away. Just occasionally an anonymous ship would appear on the distant horizon, but apart from that, there was nothing to disturb us. Indeed, if anything we were the disturbers with our football or rounders or whatever. Come the time when teatime called and we packed up and made for home. It was on these return journeys when we could speed past the dreaded cottage. No bravado needed here!

It was on a solo run to the beach that I had a dreaded puncture. These happened frequently on our country roads so I was well prepared with my tyre levers and puncture outfit. That was not the problem. The trouble was the location, right outside Jean Blaine's cottage. I looked at the bike and I looked at the cottage debating with myself, "Should I wheel it to the top of the hill for the repair, or not?" This was decided for me. I could hear the creak of a door opening.

"You, laddie!" a very loud voice exclaimed. The local seagulls scattered in a smoke-like cloud at this competition and I turned round in panic to view the figure standing in the doorway. This must be fabled Jean Blaine. There before me was a spikey haired figure in a voluminous outfit and men's black boots. "Come and help me with this bucket."

What could I do? I couldn't flee and leave my beloved bike behind. Nor could I be brave and face this phantom, if that's what it was.

"Hurry up, laddie;" and with that she turned back inside.

I gritted my teeth and sweating profusely, I faced my adventure. At the door, I could see vaguely into the interior. There was an aroma of burning peat and I could see suspended over the fire what looked like a cauldron, only a little cauldron. A shadow approached with a battered old pail and held it out.

"Here, take these ashes and dump them in the midden at the end of the garden." Again the gulls scattered at the sound.

Dutifully I grabbed the pail and made for the midden. To me, the ash appeared unusual for it seemed almost white and blew about everywhere in the light breeze. The ash at home was quite different coming as it did from a coal fire. Even so if this was from peat, it still appeared unique. Reaching my destination, I upended the bucket only to be enveloped in a choking smog as I spluttered backwards. I could feel the wretched stuff clinging to my sweaty face. I coughed my miserable way back to the cottage with the empty pail.

A giant guffaw greeted my return and the wry comment, "Never throw into the wind, laddie," more laughter and "You'd better come in and wash your face."

Seeing me hesitate, she grabbed my arm, pulled me in and stuck a wet sponge in my face. After a few minutes under a tap of cold water, I suppose I was more or less presentable, but there was no mirror to check my condition. I had my first real opportunity to examine my surroundings.

It was dark in the house, not the pitch variety, blurring the various items in the room. There was an assortment of bowls of different shapes and sizes containing an array of mysterious items, mainly plants; I couldn't identify any newts' eyes or frogs' toes in the dim light. Dark drapes hung over windows; I suppose there were windows though it was difficult to tell. Items dangled from the rafters, essentially plants such as onions and flowering twigs with an occasional string like fibre. An old-fashioned porcelain sink with a single spigot and a perpetual drip occupied a remote corner.

Jeannie shoved a jam-smeared scone into one hand and a drink into the other with, "That'll keep you going for a bit. That's raspberry jam and a bramble drink, all from the wilds." Who am I to refuse a jam scone?

She could see that something was bothering me; and it was. I was still puzzling over the white ash. "What was that stuff I dumped in the midden? It looked real funny, not like the ash at home." Perhaps it was too bold to ask.

"What's that, laddie. I'm a bit deaf, ye ken."

So I repeated a bit louder, "What was the stuff in the bucket."

Jeannie Bain paused and had a good think. Maybe I had gone too far. "Oh that. Those are the remains of people's dreams, their ambitions, their hopes – gone to join all the others in a delusion to that great reverie of nothingness."

I grunted in acknowledgement, not understanding a word and shuffled uncomfortably. I felt I had dallied enough.

"I'll have to go now and mend that puncture. Then I'll be off home. It's near my teatime." Food again!

Jeannie watched from the open door as I fetched my bike from the hedge bottom and got to work; valve out, levers round the rim, inner tube entrails pulled out, locate puncture, a wee rub with sandpaper, glue and patch applied, French chalk scraped and rubbed over, the lot replaced and a little effort with my pump; I was ready to return home.

Just as I was setting off, Jean Blaine called out from the witch's house, "Come again laddie," and I waved farewell.

Somehow I felt curious about the witch's house. I wanted to know more and a few days later I arranged to return. I said nothing about the house to my parents or my pals, for this was to be my secret; it would be my adventure and mine alone.

Again I cycled and arrived at the cottage only to be met by Jeannie herself. It was almost as though she had anticipated my arrival, so I put on my *just happened to be passing* expression, fooling no one. The greeting was friendly enough with, "Hullo, laddie. Good to see you again. I'm just collecting some wild garlic for my tea. I'm going to make some hazel stew with some of last year's nuts. You can have a helping, if you like."

A shiver and a shake of the head was answer enough. Anyway, I had to get back around 5pm for my own tea. I dismounted and advanced to see the garlic even though I could smell it from a hundred paces.

"I see you are interested in such things, laddie." She invariably called me *laddie*. "There are loads of things for eating in these woods, nuts, fruit, herbs and all sorts of leaves." I was taking in all this and tucking it away in my mind. I was sure that there was information here that would useful in future adventures.

"I keep clear of the livestock though. Any rabbits or hedgehogs or snakes or fish or birds ... they're all safe from me. And they seem to know it judging by their frequent visits."

Thus began Jeannie's instruction in natural history.

Before I left for home that afternoon, there was one question I had to ask.

"Mistress Jean, could you tell me if it's true? They say that you're a witch."

She gave one of her monstrous guffaws. "A hundred years ago they would have ducked me in the local pond, or burned me at the stake; but no. I just pretend to be because of the peace and quiet it brings;" and she went off chuckling to herself. I don't think it was cackling, yet it was difficult to tell.

That summer, my education in nature expanded greatly; the various plants, good and bad, the ones to eat, the others to use in other ways; for some had medicinal properties known since ancient times. That little white flower has roots that have a nutty taste; other ones add piquancy to soups and stews. Marigolds can be added to salads together with nasturtium seeds. I prefer mince and potatoes, myself, but I'll keep that under my hat. Timid animals browsed undisturbed in Jean's garden, fauns and rabbits and smaller creatures hidden in the undergrowth. Meat eating wildlife was discouraged.

All too soon the many days of my summer holidays drifted away and it was time for me to move on to other distractions. This was when I would be leaving the village school and accustomed friends to new faces and exciting places. I would be going to the Big School ten miles distant. That last day, I cycled to the cottage to bid my farewells and to thank Mistress Blaine for opening my eyes to my surroundings. Arriving there, I felt uneasy even embarrassed for I had no idea how to express my thanks. No doubt Jeannie Blaine had anticipated this time, for I had been talking of little else over the past week, my travel to the new school, my new friends and all the new subjects I would be studying.

As I was thinking of departing and fetched my bike, I hesitated for a long moment. Jeannie could tell the hour had come and I think I could detect a tear there.

"You'll be going then, laddie. Off you go! And remember to drink in the sights and knowledge of your new world."

With that we gave each other a big hug and she turned quickly to pass into her cottage. Slowly I cycled my way home.

Not long after, our family moved house to the Big Toon and, what with my new surroundings and fresh acquaintances, my past life faded into vague memories. Jeannie's influence was still there although I wasn't conscience of it. I kept my eyes and my mind open to all that was new. Each experience was a new adventure to be enjoyed. I took up new interests and my love of the great outdoors featured large, just enjoying discovering our world.

Jean Blaine and that part of my life now seems like a vague memory. Even so, there are times when some little incident triggers a past experience. It may simply be the brush of bracken on a walk in the hills, or the scent of white garlic flowers in a woodland wander, the perfume of burning peat, and I am reminded of the White Witch. Obediently I feast on the delights of my surroundings. That rocky mountain yonder with the waterfall streaming down its features becomes the granite face of a giant with a white beard. That loch far below reflects the upside down land of another world.

Thus lingering in my subconscious for all time will be my very own witch, Jean Blaine; for I do believe that truly, she was a witch, yet not from the West.

A MOUNTAIN OF SILVER

THIS HAPPENED SOME TIME AGO when I had more energy – a lot more energy – and spent much of my leisure time roaming the hills of Scotland. My friend Peter often accompanied me and the time had come when we had to decide where to holiday that year.

We used the usual method known as the pin-and-closed-eyes. The pin landed on a remote area in the North West Highlands, Knoydart to be exact, sort of. The reason for going there? No roads and so no populace. I suppose it was the sense of adventure, the feeling that we were exploring such a remote area. Little did I know that I personally would experience a most peculiar phenomenon on this venture.

In the list of things to take, by far the largest part was the food. I had no idea that two individuals could consume such vast amount. THINKS: "Are we going to carry all this?" UNTHINKS. As the items collect and the floorboards buckle, I get a certain uneasy feeling. As it happens, we did manage to stow everything into two rucksacks and a haversack. Our only refuge was a very old and very small tent of Egyptian cotton which would keep out most of the rain. From past experience, there would be a mist inside the tent during any showers – all very Caledonian.

Two of Peter's friends would lift us (and our gear) by car to approximately the appropriate area, the south end of Loch Quoich. From there we would hike to the lower end of Sgurr na Ciche using an access road along the side of the loch, according to the map.

The journey there took us across a misty Rannoch moor, that great bleak cold place where everything seemed dead and sodden. Even more dreary on such a day as this with the glowering sky, and 'no muckle drouth' in the grey, grey mist which hung about everywhere caressing every contour, every rotten tree stump, every peat hag. Even the bog myrtle lent gloom to the place, for the mist had distorted the slender sprigs into an army of ghostly skeletons swaying to and fro to the lament of the whining wind – voices of the past. Half seen memories sprang from the mouldering peat bog clawing at our vehicle as it passed. I was beginning to have second thoughts about our destination. Is this a manifestation of things to come!

A downward gradient took us down into a misty Glencoe; I could see why it was called Glencoe, the Glen O'Weeping. And so on to escape such surroundings, we reached Glencoe village, Ballachullish and the sea. Through Fort William and soon we were speeding along the shores of Loch Garry and a brighter day. Breaks showed in the clouds above and occasionally a lighter grey ceiling presented itself.

Our destination was just in sight, the long Loch Quoich with a kind road to take us to a place for our first camp. But wait a little! What has happened to the 'kind road'? The map had fibbed; or I should say, it was out of date; for recently, a dam had been built and the rising water now covered the road. Damn the dam!

To try to avoid the long rough trek along the side of Loch Quoich, we decided to take the shorter walk up and over the ridge – mistake! The way was steep, no wind to cool us and soon we were panting. Clothing was discarded and dangled from the packs as we slowly gained altitude. Perhaps it would have been easier to skirt the shore after all.

On and on we strode till the end of the loch was reached. By this time both of us were exhausted and to keep our spirits up we discussed food and the menu for the evening. That's when I spilled the beans and confessed to Peter that we were carrying 11 (eleven) {XI} tins of fruit. He collapsed on the spot and started rolling all over. This may have been in agony or just good humoured writhing, I don't know; anyway all that fruit was eaten before the week was over.

In all this vast wilderness, camping sites seemed to be rather hard to come by. Eventually we found a reasonably dry spot and chose to pitch our tent on what appeared to be a sandy path with a high sheltering bank to one side. The camping site proved to be ideal, indeed most comfortable.

There above us was the great bulk of the mountain silhouetted against the failing light. In the entrancement, we sat there listening to the night sounds, the trickle of a nearby stream and the lapping of the loch. There was little else. Slowly a great yellow cheese rose between a break in the surrounding hills and swung into the heavens. A full moon emerged to bewitch us.

Next morning, I opened my eyes to the pale green world

of the tent. Slowly, the noises of the outside penetrated my still-numb brain, the hiss of wind through the coarse reeds, the rivulet of a nearby stream. The mist was still down on the hills. Slowly the greyness retreated and broke into a gentle brown; and there towering over us was a Mountain of Silver set in a honey of mist. It was that magnificent Munro, Sgùrr na Cìche.

Now the mountain sparkled in the full glory of the sun and the magic of our surroundings soon became apparent. The whole ambience of the place invaded our being and brought another dimension to all its colours, its sounds, its perfumes.

Our trek through the lush green of the foothills soon gave way to shorter, more wiry grass as we gained altitude. Everywhere, there was an abundance of wild flowers of all colours - a yellow-orange spiked flower, a violet coloured miniature iris, tiny white four-petalled flowers, brilliant scarlet rock lichen, emerald green moss - everywhere there was colour. And from the thyme and bog myrtle there drifted that wonderful perfume associated with the Scottish hills.

Climbing through this pleasant area, we reached the first summit. Surroundings were bleak with outcrops of white quartz and grey granite and there, separated from us by a saddle, stood the majesty of our Mountain of Silver sparkling in the bright sunlight. Already I could feel the magic in the air as we rounded the ridge over great blocks of granite onto the flank of the mountain. A narrow ridge took us onto the summit with its massive outcrops like giant accretions of crystalline silver sparkling in the sun. Playful clouds raced at us, lifting at the last minute to go whizzing past.

As I gazed at Loch Hourn in the distant northwest, I fell

into a dream. I imagined I could see the history of the place passing down the Sound of Sleat, running with the falling tide. In former times, this stretch of sea has seen the passage of many different craft and in my dream, I could see them all; the coracles of the Picts spinning sometimes in complete circles with the vagaries of the rips; the long ships of the Viking King Haakon IV on their way to Largs and to defeat; the Warships of James IV with their proud rigs and pennants from their rigging; a lost and bedraggled galleon from the Spanish Armada entering the stormy seas of the Little Minch only to be wrecked in the Sound of Mull; even a nuclear submarine cutting a corner and running aground on a shale bank. Is Loch Hourn really Loch Hell? And did Saucy Mary actually demand tolls from all this nautical traffic? I digress and my mind wanders as I confuse these fortunes. Events merge into one conglomeration of nonsense and all fades into the pale blue mists of the Sound.

I was roused from my dwam by a tug to my sleeve. "Time to go back," Peter said.

I never did revisit the passing mirage.

PERCEPTIONS

It's funny how we view different happenings, different events from different points of view governed largely by our own prejudices. The police know this only too well when gathering witness statements after a car accident. Even colours of cars can be mistaken. No doubt, after more serious incidents such as wars, views are distorted by the historian's political affiliations. Of course they are. The writer must have some point of reference to start from even if it is, "… and I said to Montgomery, it's like this Monty …"

So it was in November, the darkness of the night was complete, no street lights, no brightly lit house windows. Only the Milky Way to break the velvet of infinity when I noticed a scratch in the heavens, a white scratch which quickly disappeared. Ah, a meteorite I thought. I'll make a wish and I made my way to the celebrations. However, there was another interpretation of the scratch.

The Seekers came from outer space and their aim in this mission was to investigate strange phenomena in the various planets around this sun. We would recognise these planets, for we live on one of them; we live on the third planet from the sun; it is Earth. This is our system. We do not know that these aliens are there for we cannot see them, just an occasional flash - a scratch in the heavens - when they happen to collide with space debris. Why is this? In spite of our vast technical knowledge, we cannot see them because they travel faster than the speed of light, indeed much faster. Perhaps it is something to do with black holes and their ability to 'swallow' light; have they managed to harness the power of neutrinos? Not only that, they have the ability to travel from Glasgow to Alice Springs in one billionth of a blink of an eye; not as you might expect by travelling around the earth's circumference, but by penetrating through the interior of the planet. It is like one gigantic cosmic conjuring trick – now you see it – now you don't.

At present, the Seekers are investigating strange happenings on Planet Earth although no doubt they have their own name for Earth. They have noted that Earth has a regular cycle, a cycle that we call a year (or thereabouts) and their investigation is currently centred on the area we call Great Britain. Over several years, they have observed aggression that recurs at the same time, in the same place and in each cycle when Virgo moves into Libra. There seems to be conflict characterised by many brightly coloured explosions, some solely white, others red and others green. Using their sophisticated laboratory facilities and spectral analyses, these show that the white is based on iron, the red on strontium and the green on barium. There is even an occasional lilac flash of calcium.

These flare ups are generally confined to the same regions during each cycle and careful examination of these regions reveal very little, very localised damage. This is strange for not so long ago (75 cycles, to be precise) two great and devastating explosions were observed on an archipelago in the same hemisphere about one third cycle removed.

Captain's Note: *Therefore these creatures certainly have the ability to cause great damage but seem reluctant to do so. This localised and rather brief battle is apparently limited to the same location each cycle. We have interpreted this as some sort of local rebellion by the general populace but we have no means of further investigation. Perhaps some future expedition can study this further and I shall file this under pending.*

The Seekers continue to investigate similar phenomena on the Third Planet of the system and have discovered an even greater mystery which occurs regularly on a much wider scale. These are similar flare-ups occurring Earth wide. The peculiar aspect of these is that they happen sequentially and progress around the planet within one rotation. They can only deduce that there is a coordinated uprising worldwide during the dark solstice. Again, there seems to be little or no co-lateral damage.

Captain's report to HQ: *We continue, as Seekers, to move from one location to another to investigate different events of interest, but the crew is turning restless with the monotony of the large areas of green. As you know, this part of the spectrum causes considerable pain to the viewing personnel and they are unable to relax during rest periods.*

As director of this project, therefore, I would like to propose that we move to another, and more interesting planet in this group. It occurs to me that the Red Planet shows much more unusual phenomena (and kinder light emissions) which would be worth exploring. My colleague, X532YZB, has observed structures there which suggest construction of vast canal systems in the recent past although this has yet to be confirmed.

The space craft with the Seekers moves on.

As for us on earth we continue to commemorate Guy Fawkes on the 5th of November with our gaily coloured fireworks of red, green and white and enjoy the green spaces on our planet. And each year when we reach the dark solstice, we celebrate as did our ancestors, only we do it with fireworks of various hues.

Meanwhile scientists, deep within an Alpine mountain in some vast man-made tunnel, try their best to detect neutrinos.

And what of the Seekers in their spaceship? Yes! They went on to explore the Red Planet, trying to justify so-called canals. Unfortunately on one of their trips through the interior of Mars, their neutrino energized craft lost power resulting in their craft materialising within, trapped in a sepulchre of stone walls hundreds of miles thick.

THE MINDWRITER

In some ways, I suppose I could be called an electronic engineer, yet I wouldn't presume to be an expert. Really my field of expertise lies in the interpretation of electronic signals and because of this, I have been assigned the Mindwriter Project. The ultimate aim is to convert signals into words. This, of course, has been done before where signals from a keyboard are converted to letters on an electronic screen. My project is rather different in that it aims to convert signals from the human brain to words on a screen. Just think, once I have ironed out the problems, you will be able to write your 100,000 word Magnum Opus in one morning

My initial approach is to trace the history of writing and to use these building blocks to construct some sort of logical basis, to give me a starting point for my project. So firstly, I must trace the origin of words and their recording through the ages.

Since the beginning of time as we know it, it has been evident that man has wanted to leave some sort of record of his being. The form of the record is to a large extent controlled by the materials available together with the technology available. It all started with a hard stone on a softer stone to produce a picture usually related to his life. From this he moved on to symbols known to a wider circle of his buddies, made by a tool perhaps a pointed stick, on a page such as a clay tablet or even on a papyrus. Sophistication bloomed and the pointed stick became a quill, then a metal nib using an ink on paper – to the fountain pen, to the Biro that coincided with illegible writing. Certain mechanical aids were invented such as the typewriter and the script became legible again. And where are we today with our tablets (not clay), desktop computers and other electronic devices! We are still looking for the next technological advance and that's where I come in.

Thus, I am engaged in the development of the latest technological toy which I am going to call a Mindwriter (analogous to typewriter). With this, the operator merely has to think of a phrase or a word for that word to appear on a page or a screen or some sort of visual device. Since the mind works so much more quickly than any manual tool, it means that writing any document such as a book will be almost instantaneous.

At present, I am only halfway through this project and have already come against certain problems which I have to resolve before this device becomes viable. The apparatus is simply a headset with various pressure pads which are attached to the head (and thence the brain). This gizmo is attached in turn to the latest in computers and it is in the development of the relevant program which is the main element of my research. I have reached the stage of being able to read brainwaves and convert these into writing which appears on a screen.

It is easy enough capturing brain waves but my system must be such that I can control the appropriate thoughts into recognisable words; indeed, did we think in terms of words or in more complex structures such as emotions? To start with, I tried a series of simple pictures picking up the impression using the eyes. Of course, all I got was the visual electronic signal to the brain, not a simple one-word signal. The picture of a banana became a yellow thing like a curved cucumber. I should have known that that approach was a non-starter.

My next try was deliberately to think the sounds of words passing, so to speak, through my head. I would imagine a voice speaking in some sort of monotone in my brain. I used the established computer program for converting word sounds to letters on a screen. This combination worked remarkably well and was certainly faster than using the voice to screen alone.

As I see it, I am now up against two major problems:

a) What I term as spam;

b) Dividing the text into words.

The control of the operation of the brain is difficult, for thoughts frequently wander away at a complete tangent. One minute I'll be thinking of the technicalities of the program in hand and suddenly it goes off thinking 'what am I going to have for lunch?' or 'Oh no, next door is cutting his grass again!' Not only that; I use the same computer to receive my e-mails and for some reason, they also appear in my text. So much for SPAM!

The second difficulty is, there is no space between the various words. Now, this got me thinking. Who invented words? After all, we don't speak words, we speak phrases. Only robots speak in words. I decided to investigate this by looking back in history and where better to start but with the Rosetta

Stone. The hieroglyphics tell us nothing so I discarded that section; but the Demonic and the Greek are both texts using their own letters – but no spaces. Roman inscriptions on, for example the plinth of statues, have no spaces between words. So when did words first appear? In the Lindisfarne Gospels of around 8th century AD, there are breaks but not between words but between the phrases used in plainchant to guide the monks in their music. Going to the Magna Carta of 1215, there are breaks between words so the practice seems to have entered regular use in documents by then.

Now my task seems to be, where and how do I insert the blanks? Back to the voice-to-text program.

The conversion of mind words to sound words seemed to be progressing and I have managed this with several simple words but even at this stage various problems cropped up. Perhaps this has something to do with local accents, yet I didn't understand how this could happen with just words in the mind.

The main trouble was the program from thoughts to sound words. The impulses from the brain to trigger words in sound, was the stumbling block. Once this is solved, I would be able to complete the triangle by connecting this to the established link of sound words to text words. My idea was to miss out the intermediate step, thus giving thought-word-to-text.

This was becoming more difficult than I thought, for all types of other unwanted signals were roaming around; these were picked up and the whole lot was turning into a real jungle. Trying to turn this lot into some sort of recognisable screen picture was well nigh impossible and the whole idea was turning into a mess big enough to send me mad. I need to develop some sort of mind filter. More and more I can identify expletives in the screen picture.

The visual picture I present is not a pretty one. There I am with this ridiculous head set, wires and pads all around, a bottle of the best malt whiskey at my elbow and the air thick with sweary words. That figure slowly slumps into an alcohol related slumber with an overtone of grunts and groans.

The sleep was not one of relaxation. All sorts of nightmares barged through my brain leaving a trail of torment and dreads that I thought were long forgotten. In the eddies of the wake, the histories of past ordeals became vivid visions of reality, of tortures and pain. I felt that I must have screamed in my wretchedness, but no-one came to my rescue. I was all alone in my anguish. This continued on and on for what seemed like drowning in a lifetime. Perhaps it was a lifetime. They say that a person drowning in water relives visions of their entire life. That was me. I was reliving my whole life. Yet, this recall appeared to be selective for my echoes were solely threatening and disagreeable. It was not a balanced equation of my past. Surely I had pleasant experiences too; yet I couldn't recall one. On and on with colours bright and garish in all sorts of unrecognisable shapes, yet terrifying, for all that. Suddenly, all went blank and my whole world imploded to nothingness.

I must have been some time later when I returned to this planet with a raging thirst and dripping sweat. My head felt constricted and it was then that I realised I was still wearing that ridiculous helmet with the electrode pads. Off with the headgear and all felt almost normal again. It was then that I noticed the screen of the computer. It had been operating all this time and there it was, a display of text from top to bottom. Not just that, the information display indicated that its size was enormous running into gigabytes.

Stunned, I spent some time just gazing at the computer screen. It just didn't make sense and the reason why was obvious; the text had no spaces. I scrolled to the top of the document trying to grasp some sort of meaning but the gobbledegook was complete rubbish. It was only when I examined the other end of the document that I realised that the text ran chronologically. This was my most recent conversation finishing with some gibberish, no doubt the result of my drunken stupor.

As a matter of interest, I tried to interpret this end drivel. It was not drivel but a series of incantations, words that are usually associated with the supernatural, with spells and the like. The psychedelic illusions were all part of the absurdity of the experience.

I am rapidly approaching the winding up of this research project and am forever wondering where we are going in this world of ours. Everything must be done faster. We go from A to B faster and knock off 2 minutes from a 24 hour journey. So what! Now I have been told what my next project will be. It will be the reverse of this current nonsense. The powers-that-be want me to devise a system whereby the written word can be transferred into brain impulses in order to speed up the reading of documents. This, of course, means that you will be able to read *War and Peace* in 2 seconds flat.

Someone! Hand me that bottle of Bruichladdich.

CRAIGLEA MISSION

I ENJOY WALKING THESE HILLS, the wide expanses that stretch the eye, clear air to cleanse the lungs with perfumes of myrtle, the whispers of the grasses, the frequent rains that seek their way under collar and down the spine. Today is one of those days – frequent showers with bright periods. I look forward to the bright periods.

I had just finished brewing up in the shelter of a sheep rhea and nibbled away at a soggy sandwich, corned beef I think, when my mind turned to the story of these parts. Over the years, colourful history had been enacted in these hills. Kennedy was the big name here and there are many dark tales linked to the clan in this Galloway district, yet these in no way overshadow other local histories. Bruce had a famous victory over Edward I (of England) in Glen Trool. This was the main stomping ground of the Covenanters. The Raiders of S. R. Crocket roamed over these hills. Many a hero of John Buchan's novels tramped this sodden turf.

Time to head for a suitable camping site and it certainly wasn't here in the open Galloway hills. I had to push further down and off this wet pitch and onto drier land. My route took me over the Rhinns of Kells to what seemed to be a more arable area, but not a region I was too familiar with. The map also showed various woodlands which would give some shelter from the freshening wind. However, great anvils of storm clouds were starting to form on the windward side and would surely find me in my semi-sodden state so I must hurry and pitch my tent.

Passing a stand of birches, I caught sight of a lone building on a slight rise. It was just as the storm caught me, a mere few drops to start but larger drops foretelling heavier rain to come. I detected a distant rumble, not of corned beef sandwiches but of thunder and I didn't fancy being near the trees when there was lightning about. I hurried to the building which seemed to be some sort of church. Along its front there was a faded marker displaying "Craiglea," and more to the point, there was a porch which would give some shelter till the storm passed.

Once in the portal, I could hear the drumming on its corrugated iron roof as the storm finally made its full presence felt. Water splashed in the doorway giving a fine misty spray. Although a shelter of sorts, this porch was no place to spend the night. I tried the door. It was unlocked and I entered.

Inside, all was calm except for the drumming of the rain; for the church – I assumed it was a church – was also roofed in corrugated iron. The consuming sound was such that all other sounds were cloaked. I was inside a great chamber of much sound which would not permit any competition. I just sat in a pew, put fingers in ears and looked around me.

Yes! I was right. This was a church, or had been, for the place looked forlorn, dusty and neglected. It seemed abandoned to the elements long ago. There were rows of pews in two parallel sets facing a lonely forgone lectern and a sole wooden cross on the wall. All around the walls was a wainscot of tongue and groove pine. The plaster on the upper wall was suffering from the damp surroundings and a patch had broken away exposing the underlying lath. The remains of a pot-bellied stove stood in the corner behind the lectern. There was a door at the other corner, probably leading to a cupboard.

For all its neglect, the property seemed sound enough so it must have been deserted for some other reason – the drumming out of the sermons by the frequent rains, perhaps; or a better church elsewhere; or just that the congregation had dwindled or moved to another area.

Moving around to keep warm, I explored the various nooks and crannies of the main body of the kirk but discovered nothing of interest. All the while, the drumming of the rain continued to invade my senses and I wondered if I would ever hear again. Opening the door at the corner, I turned on my LED torch only to reveal further neglect. There was a deal table with a stack of hymn books, some papers, a squab or bolster of Black-Watch tartan and a bundle of sticks. All were decorated with a century-thick layer of dust. The remains of a dead bird lay on the floor, a victim of the holy place yet a touch of reality to the scene. There wasn't much joy in this corner of religion. I closed the door of the bird's tomb.

Returning to my pack, I squeezed back in the pew while night was closing in. In an instant, the drumming stopped just as suddenly as it had started. I pulled out my sleeping bag with the intention of keeping warm and used my light to add to the illusion and for a time I dozed. Without warning, the post-storm silence was shattered by a scream so bloodcurdling as to make hair on the back of my neck bristle. It came from the anteroom. Someone had snuck in under darkness and was trying to scare me. They were successful.

"I'll put a stop to this," I thought and leapt forward towards the outer room. Before I reached it, the door flew open to reveal a strange glow from within and there, outlined against the light there stood a set of wailing bagpipes. The pipes seemed to step forward on its drones and into the body of the kirk, all the time playing a dirge of a pibroch. The glow moved with them. The chanter drooped and the sound slid down to silence. I just stood there dumbfounded.

That was not the end of the matter. Up with the chanter and the wailing invaded my senses once more, this time with a reel. That was not all, for the drones swept through the air, the pipes leaped and *pas de bas*'d through the air in time to the dance. Round and round it whirled, back and forth with great skips and jumps and bounds till I was dizzy yet enthralled at the same time. I tapped my boots along with the rhythm embroiled with the dancing aura of the twirling pipes.

The sound crescendoed to a frenzied shriek, back and forth over the space carrying the glow with it. The rafters rang with the skirl; the pipes clamoured yet louder and bellowed and bawled; my boots stamped out with a life of their own; my whole body twisted and turned with every cadence, pulse and throb. I no longer had a body to be aware of. And the tune moved seamlessly into a slip jig with its three-stem rant. Drone stalks stuck out at all angles as the pipes whirled round and round in a strange pattern all fast and furious or no pattern at all until all dance was chaos. All loud and louder still!

An abrupt thunder stopped all. Another heavy downpour hit the tin roof drowning all in its boom. The light vanished. The anteroom door thudded shut and I gathered up my gear and got out into the drenching rain double quick. I ran.

Morning light was showing as I found a metalled highway and by the time I reached the village about a mile distant, it was fully daylight. Sheltering my dripping self under the awning of the village shop, a wifie within opened the door enquiringly.

"The old church up the hill ..." I asked?

"Och! The old Mission Hall," she interrupted. "That's long gone. They knocked it down years ago - said it was haunted."

A TALE OF THE SEA

The sea is a fickle beast; one minute it is serene, the next like the end of everything. Despite all its moods, mankind is drawn to the sea. People long to retire to that little cottage by the briny with the perpetual sound of the ocean, its calming effect and tranquillity. Yet it can be frightening too, when gales sweep in to rouse the waters to mountains, green to the eye, topped with foam, to dash all before to tiny smithereens. Such power inspires the poet and the songwriter, the landscape Turners and Rembrandts. But just as readily, they may be turned by reflections on an ocean mirror.

Personally, I have a sort of love/hate relationship with the sea. I long to feel beneath my feet the sensation of a vessel over waves, the graceful movement dipping and rising with an occasional spindrift over the prow. The odd thing is that I have never learned to swim and therefore have no inclination to enter the sea, neither deliberately nor accidently. Occasionally I have been drenched by a delinquent wave and on one occasion I did land in the water when my dingy overturned.

On one of my love-the-sea cruises, we were heading for home. The vessel was a 70ft mv, a former rescue ship of the

Norwegian fishing fleet. It took us swiftly past the Kyle of Lochalsh on a falling tide and into Kyle Rhea with a brief glimpse of Loch Duich and later, the wide opening of Loch Hourn – don't the place names trip off a tongue pretending to be knowledgeable. Just west of Loch Hourn on the Skye side lies the tiny island of Ornsay providing a favourite natural harbour. There, we planned to spend the night sheltered from the promised storm.

The following day, we took a southerly line and braved the high winds astern and although the winds did materialise, the wave formation was rather curious and not as wild as anticipated. The seas were certainly large yet with no broken tops or untamed spindrift. The result was a smooth up-and-down with a long frequency which all made for an agreeable voyage helped by the boat's stabilizers. We overtook a working fishing boat, not so lucky, wallowing in the swell. A blond gannet passed with some purpose unrevealed to us mere mortals; I guess it was thinking of fish suppers, what else. The sea was being kind.

My mind drifted to other things as time slipped past and I recollected a tale told to me by a Shetland friend. He assured me it was true and I believe him. The event happened away back in the late 19th century, in Queen Victoria's reign. This concerned a lady, by name Betty Mouat who lived on a farm on South Mainland, Shetland. She made a living working on the farm, sewing and knitting, shawls mainly.

You could say that Betty Mouat was accident prone or just unlucky. When still quite young, she had been accidently shot in the head. She had a bad limp, the result of a cart running over her foot and she had a mild stroke when she was sixty. The resultant difficulties prompted her to seek medical advice in Lerwick.

Betty's home was in a remote farm on the peninsular of Scatness (near Sumbrough) and was about 25 miles from Lerwick and although that would be no problem for a fit Shetlander to walk, she had this difficulty with her crippled foot. It was decided, then, to take the sea route from the harbour at Grutness, a difficult voyage at that time of year for it was then well into January.

Accordingly, Betty boarded the sailing vessel, *Columbine* to sail north to Lerwick just as a storm from the south was brewing. She was duly ensconced in the cabin although she had to be helped down the boat's rickety steps because of her gamy leg. The vessel cast off and was just under way when the sheet to the mainsail parted, the boom swung round and the skipper landed in the sea. In an effort to save him, the two crew members jumped in and all were swept away.

By this time, the *Columbine* had crossed the bar and was caught up by the southerly only to be dragged into the wild grey confusion of the North Sea. As the craft swirled randomly in the chaos of the waves, Betty called out in vain as she was buffeted around in the cabin. There was no way she could mount the steps, nor did she wish to and she slumped back onto the bench and started to pray.

Columbine continued to drift northwards stern first, further and further from the safety of the Shetland Isles and into the gloom of the long January night. The sails of the vessel had long been ripped and blown away with the remains of the rigging trailing in the waters. All night long the roar of the wind churned the seas causing vast areas of spindrift to float past and over the bows of the boat. The boat now a poor shadow of its original proud contours, no longer the dove of the sea, struggled on in its erratic voyage northwards to a destiny still concealed. And all the time, Betty clasped her shawl around while holding a jar of milk and some pathetic very damp biscuits.

Grey daylight emerged to disclose no change in the situation. The wind continued its relentless gale; the boat continued its relentless way; time just continued.

By the fourth day, the storm had moderated somewhat yet the little craft continued to drift north in a grey North Sea raising some little hope, though the violent movement of the sea continued. Through the hatch of the cabin, Betty could see a vision of unrelenting grey and more grey with the sky barely above the sea mountains; no seagulls to talk to, not even an albatross.

Betty nibbled the damp biscuits out of boredom more than hunger. Her jar of milk had since soured and been tipped into the bilges. All she had to drink was some collected rain in that same jar. The rain had seeped through the sprung boards of the cabin ceiling and no doubt the skin of the boat would be suffering too.

By the sixth day, the storm had returned with increased ferocity. The tops of the water mountains sparkled white with foam which blew away to the distance in long streaks. The motion of the little boat grew more erratic rattling her contents to the four corners of the little cabin. Betty Mouat was less than pleased. Her despair deepened and she feared greatly for her safety. She closed her eyes and held on; wondered what lay at the end of the ocean.

It was the seventh day; despair deepened.

The eighth appeared through the grey of the dawn. Betty Mouat peering through the open hatchway could just make out an uncompromisingly jagged outline with rocky feet drowned in enormous breaking waves. For the first time, she felt angry; angry that she had endured all this, just to be dashed against some black rocks at the end of the world. The anger welled up and burst out against the sea; "You barbarian, you devil, you fiend! You brought me all this way dangling HOPE before me just to lure me onto these rocks."

The sea blushed bright green, embarrassed. A giant swell lifted *Columbine* over the reef and safely onto the only stretch of beach on the Norwegian island of Lepsøya. So ended her voyage. There, she was rescued by a local fisherman and returned to Shetland as a celebrity.

Note: I found out later that she lived to the ripe old age of 93, dying on February 6th, 1918. It was the 32nd anniversary of her last terrible night at sea.

PAINTER OF EGGS

In my working days I made my living painting eggs; not any old eggs; these were ostrich eggs. Although I say it myself, they were works of art, perhaps not up to Fabergé standard, but I continued to paint them until some wildtrust busybody had the sale of such eggs banned. Thereafter, I retired before the Grim Reaper decided to call in my number to some egg-hole in the ground.

The Easter season is here and since I seem to have time on my hands, I have decided to revive my egg painting skills. These days, though, I shall have a smaller canvas, hens' eggs and maybe one or two ducks'. Firstly, I fill to the mark this giant tureen with water; then lots and lots of eggs, brown ones, lightly tanned ones, white ones and green ducks' eggs. I turn up the gas to high and boil the victims for twelve minutes. I'm not exactly sure why I choose twelve yet I'm sure I read this number in some ancient book of spells. The eggs are then allowed to cool.

There! I have my many blank faces awaiting their personalities. Out with the poster paints, the acrylics, some oils and even gouache. I steer clear of water colour; it is too transparent with not enough drama for my taste.

I think I'll start the batch with a variety of mouths. So often the character is determined by the mouth; a thin horizontal line for grumpy and someone who dislikes whiskey; a very wide-open gob for one about to sneeze; a coy half-smiling one for bashful – wait a minute, this is turning into the seven dwarfs. Next to the other features to establish my characters.

When I think of eyes, I feel that the complexities of the individual are exposed. After all, they say that the eyes are the reflection of the soul. I use my camel hair for the eyes, just fine lines to establish the personality. The technique is to load the camel hair with paint and twirl the brush in my lips. It makes an awful mess of my face but produces a fine point to the brush. I combine this with a dot for the pupil, essential for the disposition of the egg-character. A normal eye shape denotes normal concentration of the mind; a slit with the pupils in the corner for slyness; a round eye with pupils to the ceiling shows someone away with the fairies; with one eye closed, it's time they went to Specsavers; combined with a furrowed brow is puzzlement; added red lines indicate a heavy drinker. So I could go on with different combinations of these quirks.

Noses are somewhat more difficult. I usually just forget about noses with an occasional flaring nostril, a wart or a break. Hairstyle is different. I have much fun adding different modes to my egg models; perhaps up-swept here or side sleeked there; a centre parting, or a wide parting bald pate. Colours vary from blond to red to black to grey or none at all; perhaps one or two of the greys have a touch of purple or even green.

I add some little final touches. There are moustaches of various styles and an occasional beard, even side burns. Freckles are added to the redhead and a red nose to the boozer. There are some 'shades' for the more sophisticated and horn-rimmed for the intellectual.

With these details completed, these characters are laid aside to dry. If I get lost with too much detail, the personality will get lost in fuzzy trivia.

On top of the dresser, inherited from grandma, I have placed side by side thick slices of bread. These I will use as stands for my eggs, pressing dimples in the bread so that my friends can perch upright. The ducks' eggs can be the back row as they are the tallest; next a row of brown; more bread slices for the next row of tan and some white. I must put aside one slice for my toasted cheese supper. I seem to have one duck egg over. I'll put her at the front. Her! Have I turned into an egg sexpert?

I stand back and survey my array of characters; and they stare back. Enough! I think I deserve my toasted cheese supper.

Over the supper table I began to wonder if I have over-done my egg project. Was this just a lot of nonsense dreamt up in a spur-of-the-moment madness, another of my crazy schemes? Anyway, I had a sense of achievement so what more could I ask! It's time for bed.

That night I toss and turn for a time with my brain too active; or could it be the toasted cheese. More shuffling about, a stagger around the bedroom and a gaze from window at the mist shroud outside. It was then that I notice a peculiar sound foreign to the night. It seems to come from downstairs and certainly warrants further investigation.

I creep downstairs avoiding their many creaks and pass through the open doorway to the living room. In the gloom, there is just enough light to discern my array of eggs. They seem to be singing some sort of ancient song – very beautiful and full of the harmonies linked to the plainsong of bygone days. There at their front is the duck egg singing a solo part, a very high part (so I was right about the *she*) a part which soars away above the others. They then repeat the lot, another verse perhaps, and all in Latin. The classical language I do recognise, yet I don't realise that eggs can sing so beautifully.

Slowly and quietly I withdraw and leave the choir to their own little concert and I return to my bedroom. Perhaps I should call it my *bedchamber* to be in keeping with the occasion. The rest of the night is spent in sweet slumber.

The following day, I blamed my midnight happening on my toasted cheese and returned to my plan of hiding the various eggs in diverse hidey holes in my garden expecting rummaging children to find them sometime over this Easter period. And that, I thought, was the end of the whole affair.

Sometime later, however, while on holiday visiting various cathedrals in England, I had recall of the whole incident. I just happened to be visiting this holy place near Cambridge when I heard that same piece of music as I entered the building. Half expecting to find my egg choir as I passed inside, I looked around only to discover some group of humans had taken over the egg opus, a composition by the Italian composer, Allegri entitled *Misereri mei, Deus;* truly out of this world.

That music haunts me to this day.

THE LAST LAUGH

The Borders Philharmonic Orchestra (BPO) is a small symphony orchestra of professional musicians located in the North Country. As yet, we have not become a Big Name in the classical music world but I feel we are getting there and once we land that recording contract, we should take off. Things did take off and over time we gained a reputation, some say as a training orchestra for aspiring players, but that was just sour grapes.

At the beginning, the BPO repertoire was rather limited mainly because of the size of the Orchestra library; moreover sheet music in those days was expensive (and still is) and the cost to hire music is ludicrous. Often we are tempted to borrow from other orchestras if we can, although we often meet with some resistance; parts so often get lost in transit. The Orchestra's resident conductor is rather keen on Sibelius so our library is strong there.

Cash is a perpetual problem for the performing arts and we are no different. We have a faithful audience who support us through regular attendance at concerts but essentially we depend on grants and some support from local industry. All this disappears in wages and overheads such as concert hall fees and rehearsal space. Wages are thin, yet we realise that we are not yet established on the concert circuit. At the start, the BPO was never renowned as 'snappy dressers' for the protocol then was white shirts for the men and fresh shirts for each performance. After a half-season of shirt-washing, the protocol became white threadbare shirts. There was a huge sigh of relief when this changed to black shirts. Some players now go for a whole season on one washing, but they are forced to sit on their own. Nevertheless, we are a happy tight bunch of performers, which is not always true with other, more established orchestras and I think we can attribute this to our resident conductor, Giancomo Dorma.

Giancomo Dorma, known to the orchestra as Sleepy Jim, creates an atmosphere of enjoyment in our music making which is reflected in our performances. He is a natty dresser, neat hair (unknown in music circles) always with a coloured silk hanky draped from his breast pocket and always the welcoming smile especially for newcomers to the group. In a way, I think the youngsters starting out on their playing careers regard the BPO as a staging post to greater heights and to more established orchestras and it is mainly these ones who move on. Giancomo is happy to help them in their future careers.

As for me, I play in the viola section and expect to be there till I retire. Needless to say, we violas are the butt of all the jokes, viola jokes of course. It has been so since the 18th century (not that I'm that old) and we are well used to them. I feel that the others are just jealous of our unique alto clef and beautiful sound, though others may argue otherwise. Here is the latest viola joke: *What is the difference between a viola and an onion? No one cries when you chop up a viola*. Cruel, don't you think!

I suspect that Dorma had a previous life as a joker, for he is forever doing the most ridiculous things, childish tricks even conjuring stuff. It certainly lightens rehearsals which can be quite tense at times and all in all it does engender a devoted atmosphere among the players. There was the occasion when he placed a whoopee cushion on the leader's chair. The resultant rude noise and the orchestra's reaction engendered the appropriate mood for rehearsing *Peter and the Wolf*. On the other hand, the leader who was rather staid turned quite, what shall we say, starchy.

On another occasion after a torrid rehearsal, our conductor took his silk hanky (green) and mopped his brow dramatically. Pretending to wring the hanky, it turned red with the remark, "I sweated ze blood, there." On the whole, the PBO was a happy bunch of players and quite mad.

Season after season slipped by and the orchestra grew. Its repertoire expanded indeed it was gaining quite a reputation for its interpretation of Sibelius's work. We landed a contract with Supreme Records and even performed at the London Proms on one occasion. Time slipped past without a murmur and before we knew it, many of us were sporting grey hairs or bald pates and the years were particularly exacting for Sleepy Jim. His eye was as bright as before but his body was shrinking. He no longer cut a dashing figure as he took to the rostrum. Indeed, he was quite bent and I had the feeling that his baton lacked its former vigour.

I suppose time catches up with us all eventually and our

now quite frail Giacomo Dorma declared that this would be his final season. Towards the end of that year and into the spring of the following, we discussed what would be appropriate for a farewell concert programme. Maestro declared, "I've wanted to play something from Khachaturian's Ballet, Gayanah – oh I know it's too long to play the lot. How about starting with the Dance of the Rose Maidens. That's only three minutes or so. We could stick it in as an opener." I looked round at the vacant expressions on the faces of the music committee. They, indeed, did not know the item nor was it in the library. Still, it would be a change from some of our dusty pieces. I would make an effort to search it out. We had until the end of April before the concert and it was now only January.

"We must, of course have Sibelius," continued Giancomo; "Perhaps his 5th Symphony." Well, that was no problem. We had played it often enough and enjoyed the work; besides, it was in the library. "And lets bring in extra brass; it needs more brass," he declared. This was turning out to be an expensive final concert. "And for an encore, we'll have Valse Triste, Sibelius again. That, of course will be after the symphony." He had it all planned, then, I thought as I gazed at the other committee members.

A not-so-Sleepy Jim looked round at the others. "We have to have a concerto in the first half with a celebrity for soloist. Any ideas?"

"Frederick Carlisle, remember he used to play in our firsts; he's making quite a reputation for himself," suggested Hugo from trombones.

"A violin concerto?" thought the Maestro and then turning

to me, "Find out if he's available and which works are in his current repertoire. I myself fancy the Brahms or even the Bruch Scottish Fantasy."

Meanwhile I had been browsing through the music catalogues to see if I could find The Rose Maidens without success. I did find the suite Gayanah which includes the Rose Maidens and pointed this out to the Maestro. "We can do the whole suite," he declared. "It's only about 20 minutes and I rather like Khachaturian." So that was that.

The programme for this special event had been established without the usual arguments, the coming and going, the squabbles and deletions. Sleepy Jim had been so decisive in his choice that there was no option but to agree with his selection. So far, the line up was:

FAREWELL PROGRAMME
GAYANAH SUITE
CONCERTO
INTERVAL
SIBELIUS SYMPHONY 5
(encore – VALSE TRYSTE, SIBELIUS)

We would check the programme duration once we firmed up on the soloist and his solo item but it looked like an hour and a half playing plus five minute encore and a half hour interval, just about the standard length for one of our concerts.

Winter that year slipped away and we were rapidly approaching the special day of Giacomo Dorma's farewell concert. Carlisle, our soloist confirmed the date and the Bruch

Scottish piece. The sheet music had arrived and checked into the library; we even had a sponsor to foot that bill. Extra rehearsals were scheduled with a start this coming Tuesday.

The Orchestra started the rehearsal with the Khachaturian and much fun particularly with The Sabre Dance. The Maestro had certainly picked a winner there. My only surprise was that we hadn't played it before. The remainder of the rehearsal was spent on the symphony. Giacome even had a surprise there. I should explain that the final movement has a very dramatic end. One of the themes is played in a series of block chords so that it sounds as CHORD – SPACE – CHORD – SPACE … to the end. When we reached this part, our conductor simple raised his baton and held it there. Heedless, the orchestra continued and immediately went into free-fall with no neat block chords but with a maelstrom of cacophony. The Boss just smiled as though to say, "You need me after all!" his little joke.

The day of the Farewell Concert arrived. We titled the programme, *The Maestro's Choice*, an appropriate title, for it certainly was his choice. Usually our programmes were a consensus of the committee members, but not this time. It was his last concert, after all.

Come the evening, the audience arrived. Booking had been heavy and we could be in for a full house. The stage was all set, stands and desk lights, sheet music and celebratory programmes (in colour, no less). Contrary to our usual practice of wandering onto the stage in dribs and drabs to take our seats, we entered in regimental form starting with the brass, percussion and horns, through to lower strings, upper strings and harp, then upper strings. Pause. Restless audience which slowly settled.

Enter the Leader to mild applause. The audience quietened expectantly.

Enter Maestro Giacomo Dorma to a tumultuous ovation, all immaculate in his penguin suit complete with drooping silk handkerchief. The audience realised that this would be his last appearance. He did too and tried to straighten his drooping frame as he walked slowly to the rostrum. Baton raised and straight into the boisterous Khachaturian.

With applause still ringing, Giacomo led our soloist, Frederick Carlisle to his place between the rostrum and the Leader. A quick tuning by the soloist and we were into the delights of the concerto. With soaring notes, arpeggios and scales and passages of brilliance with Scottish tunes sprinkled throughout, we glided on through the piece. At one point there was a poignant duet with violin and harp and all ended with an arrogant Scottish statement.

The audience greeted the finale with enthusiastic applause for soloist and orchestra with special acclaim for Jeannie, the harpist; quite right too, for over the years, she seldom was recognised for her contributions.

We all trooped backstage for the interval and the mood there was one of quiet satisfaction. You could have cut the elation in the atmosphere, I think too, of fulfilment that we were bidding farewell to our conductor on a high. On the other hand, Giancomo just sat there, face pale with never a word, probably too full of emotion to comment. So unlike him! He usually bounced around dropping comments to the various cliques of players all lively with nervous energy and highly pitched voices his own voice pitched even higher.

"A great concert, Maestro," I commented in a bid to draw him if only a little. He turned his head to look at me and I think I detected a tear there. He made no comment.

The five minute bell went for the second part.

With the orchestra settling in their places, conductor Dormo hobbled to centre stage and slowly mounted the rostrum to loud applause – then utter silence. Baton raised and then fell to open slowly this great symphony, the horns proceeding with waves of liquid joined later by the strings. The music progressed, increasing in tempo all the while with lots of dark moments. Into the second movement with its chorale in various forms. Then into the fizz of the final movement and drama leading up to the final six isolated chords. What an ending! The Maestro stood stock still in silence for a few moments before dropping his arms to his side.

With thunderous applause ringing in his ears, Giacomo Dorma moved haltingly and reluctantly to the wings and disappeared from view. The clapping went on and on; they all wanted more and we all expected him to return for his encore; yet nothing happened. The members of the BPO fidgeted uneasily and peered around anticipating his re-entry – to no avail. What was the delay?

Eventually, the stage manager stepped forward from the side curtain and raised his hands for silence. He addressed both audience and orchestra: "Ladies and gentlemen – and Orchestra; I am sorry to announce that Maestro Dormo has taken ill," much murmuring and movement from the audience; great unease from orchestra members. He continued, "He requests that the Orchestra play an encore, just for him but without him."

Music on the stands was opened, the audience settled and the strains of *Valse Tryste* poured forth, quietly and sadly. At this point I should point out that near the end of the piece there is a 'general pause' marked 'GP' over a bar of music. This means that no one plays for this one bar. It is a useful device. Not just because all players know where we have reached, it also gives publishers a convenient point to have a page turn. Thus when we reached this point, we all turned the page only to be confronted with a blank sheet. The GP went on and on for it was obvious to the players what had happened; Sleepy Jim had doctored the music, his last little joke. A bewildered audience wondered why there were guffaws of laughter ringing out from the orchestra players and no ending to the waltz.

Maestro had his last laugh and smiled in the wings of the theatre.

THE DEAD FOREST

I AM A SPIRIT. IN the time of living, these islands were my home where I had a small croft managing an existence with a few hardy vegetables penned in a tiny plot, stone fenced against my few sheep intent on razing it. These were strong willed beasts. They had to be to survive the rigours of the far north and frequently they would butt my stone dyke to get at the sweet vegetables.

That was the time when these islands were battered by frequent gales, with rains drifting in from the ocean. There were long dark nights, a time to courie inside with shutters in place and peats glowing and with just occasionally perhaps, a wee dram coddled in the hand. A happy time, you might think, and happy enough.

Needless to say, there were problems; indeed, what era is without its troubles? You only have to look at a chart from that time to understand the main hassle. Up in the north section you will notice the legend *Here Be Giants* and that is the issue. Up there be the giants, Herma and Saxa who were forever quarrelling. If it weren't about land, it would be about food, or just about anything that came to mind. Typically, after a violent fisticuffs session, Herma would go off and sulk on distant Muckle Flugga, whereas Saxa would rant and rave on the upper slopes of Saxa Vord. The story goes that, one day Herma set out intent on fishing. He ripped off the mast of Old Jamie's fishing boat to use as a fishing pole and tossed the boat onto the roof of Jamie's cottage, to be seen to this day. I can vouch for that. The giant went fishing and caught a whale but had no pan to boil the catch for his supper. He asked Saxa nicely (well, nicely for a giant) if he could use his kettle. Saxa agreed but only if he could keep most of the delicious whale for himself. No way! And that started a great fight. Huge boulders were tossed at one another together with expansive insults. The giants are long gone now but their debris can still be seen; the great boiling kettle growling away and various enormous rocks scattered around.

There came the time when, by the Reaper's scythe, I left all this and entered the spirit world. Here I have given up time to explore the wider regions of these islands, to see the changes for better and for worse. There was a time in that other place when I too kept a fishing boat. It was a double ender with a gaff rig and I kept it in one of the eastern voes away from the gales. Those were in halcyon days long gone. Now the seas seem to have been annexed by immense galleys silently cutting the waves and apparently without oarsmen as far as I could discern. I seem to be haunted by giants and more giants. These monsters of the sea seem to favour one particularly deep voe and tie-up for a short period. Then they would be off again regardless of the wind's strength or direction. Too many times I have seen them near disaster as they pass closely near the skerries in the area.

Great mists gather now and envelop the south in their cheerless way, cutting out familiar landmarks and, in their own manner, familiar sounds. Caught in the witchery of this sightless, soundless world, I feel afraid of its sorcery and am relieved when they are blown away. I can again recognise the familiar rolling moorlands of these enchanted islands.

Up by one of the northern voes, there seems to be something new, or new to my eyes. It is the strangest sight for these latitudes, for it appears that this is a forest. In the living world I had never seen an actual tree although I understand there is a small grove sheltering in a southern hollow and far from the salt of the ocean. Yet that one is a poor specimen all battered ragged by howling squalls. This forest was different. The trees seemed straight and upright and regimented into a square. I must find out more and drifted down to the copse.

Even from my limited experience with trees, I could see that these were different from my perceived ideas. They grew very straight and upright and seemed to be a mixture of types; for some were thin, others medium with some quite sturdy. I drifted through this forest looking for signs of activity or life, with little success. The whole thicket seemed deserted; and yet there were various sounds which were foreign to me. Close to a tree and I could hear a high whistle. This was common to the thin ones. Perhaps it was the sound of sap passing through the stems. Yet the medium trees were quite lifeless whereas the sturdy ones seemed to bubble away almost as though their sap were boiling.

With my scant knowledge of trees, I could only guess their names. The sturdy ones were the nearest my idea of an oak tree but I was clueless about the others. They didn't fit my notion of a pine or larch whereas ash and birch were out. Another puzzle was the absence of leaves; perhaps blown off by the island gales. Most perplexing of all was the colour of the tree trunks. These seemed to be uniformly grey, not my idea of the pleasant woodlands in the books I had read. Nor were there any bluebells or primroses scenting this copse, certainly no fairyland. Even the ground was featureless, level and covered with gravel. As a spirit, I shouldn't really say this; I felt spooked. Over to one side were some fallen branches, I think, which have turned a dark brown with time just like that rusty old anchor I had for my boat. Nevertheless, these are not the picture I have of wood, for in my former life I frequently had to repair my boat and the wood I used certainly seemed different; but there you go, I am no expert in wood types.

I notice, too, that someone had painted rings around many of the trees, white ones here, red ones there and black over there. Not only that, there were letters on some; there an LP and over there, E2 and even an instruction of DOWNCOMER on another. I expect that was an instruction to the lumberjack. There is an occasional worker walking round with a pen and a board, taking notes from – what? I've only just noticed various clocks here and there stuck on the sides of some trees. He is noting the time on these various clocks – most strange!

I expect that this coppice is destined for felling and will be gone when next I waft past and their dead shapes will be a thing of the past. I was just about to explore another area when I spied a sign, a weather-beaten plaque well punished by the salt laden gales. I could just make out part of the maxim – *S-llom Voe*. It didn't mean anything to me and was quite unpronounceable.

BEN

Some time ago I had a Jack Russell which I named Ben. He was a bonny wee dog with a black patch around one eye like a pirate, a stealer of hearts; perhaps I should have called him patch, but no matter. I trained him from a pup and found him intelligent, yet all Jack Russells are probably so. At times he would look at me as though to say, "What an idiot. I'll take him for a ride." Then, off he'd race with me chasing after like a halfwit. At other times his eyes expressed sadness to fit a current mood. This all seemed natural to my way of thinking and according to my understanding of the sensitivities of doggies. Yet there were other occasions that he seemed to employ an air of mystery or even superiority, looking down his nose at all and sundry. Anyway, Ben was a great pal and would go everywhere with me, a sort of bodyguard.

It was around the time I had that little red sports car, the MG Magna. I thought, with a name like Magna, it should be a magnet for the lassies – I'm still waiting. I should point out that this was some time ago and although this model was produced in the early-1930s, it still had a lot of life in her when I owned her. This was a little two-seater with spoked wheels, twin carbs, a crash gearbox and an oil drip. It looked fast but that was just an illusion.

However, Ben had some peculiar ideas. When I said "Walkies", he would dash outside and into the passenger seat of the car, waiting there for me to join him for "walkies". I feel that at some stage in his training we had got our lines crossed. As a result of this, we would motor everywhere together and this being a two-seater, there would be no room for any lassie.

This was just at the time when seat belts were encouraged, so I had anchor points welded to the car frame. In addition to my seat belt, I had a special harness made to fit Ben. Moreover, I should explain that when the car hood is removed, my eyes water, not with emotion but with cold draughts. I therefore wear goggles for such occasions. I did think of buying a leather hat and goggles for Ben, but never got round to it. Thus it was that Ben and I were familiar figures driving round together and no doubt we provoked various comments from the populace.

I think that our favourite destination for outings was Ganavan, away north in Argyll. We would set off together to a grinding chorus of gears with our picnic box strapped to the rack over the boot and the two of us strapped to the inside. There were times when it rained, this being the Highlands, yet we managed with the hood up and the wipers screeching to and fro over a misty screen. In fair weather in the open car, we would bowl along sometimes with me singing the latest hit and Ben howling his obbligato.

The journey took us past Loch Lubnaig to Crianlarich and beyond to Tyndrum where we would stop at The Green Wellie for ice cream, one pokey hat each. After a comfort break, we would continue north, along Loch Awe shores and through Taynuilt. Sweeping grandly into Oban, we would progress slowly, very slowly, and royally in second gear along the high street with Ben duly giving a regal wave to the onlookers, a habit picked up from those damn corgis; past the North Harbour and then along the shore to Ganavan.

Time for lunch with Winalot for Ben and the ubiquitous corned beef sandwiches for me. It was a race to see who would finish first; I always lost. As a prize, Ben would cadge whatever corned beef remained and I would be left with bread and some half-licked butter. That was the cue for playtime with a barking-mad Ben hurtling down the sandy beach chasing the teasing seagulls. Meanwhile I would set about changing the six plugs which, for some reason, were oiling up. I too was oiling up with face smeared with war-paint.

Afterwards, as I relaxed flat out on a tweed rug on the beach, Ben would spend the day fetching odd pieces of driftwood in the hope that I'd play 'fetch and carry'. Occasionally, I would succumb and toss a twig or two and even get to my feet to play footy with an old ball. As usual, he would beat me every time.

With the air turning chilly, it was time to return *chez nous* for I could feel rain in the air. With the top up and both of us belted in, we were off to more pain from the gears and some sharp protests from the new plugs. The final act of the trip was to collect kippers from the Inverawa Smokery for MY tea. Ben didn't like kippers!

The years slipped by and we grew older and wiser – just a little. Gone was the sports car and its temperament, to be replaced by a more sedate Triumph Herald with its own problems. Often I look back nostalgically to those early days and dutifully take my keep-alive pills. I think that Ben too would recall those halcyon days and sigh.

One dark and particularly stormy evening, Ben and I had just returned from our comfort stroll. I was settling in my soft armchair by the log fire with a glass of *deoch-slainte* when Ben gave one of his customary groans and a big stretch. At the time, I thought nothing of it and duly dozed off. The whiskey swirled around my brain as ever and my mind was filled with all the colours of a psychedelic rainbow.

I drifted into a dream-world that was strange to me. There, all around, was a vast display of sand, not like Ganavan but the sharp, coarse grains of the desert. In the distance, I could make out lush greenery of a kinder country and I had a longing to be there within the cool of its vegetation; for all around was this strange heat of an arid desert. Even in my dream my senses told me that this could not be.

In the distance towards the green land I could make out a quill of smoke or dust. It seemed to be coming my way. The blue-grey of distance became more defined as the dust came nearer and soon I could distinguish what seemed to be a chariot pulled along at break-neck speed by two black horses. Even closer I could see that the chariot was coloured bright red, reminiscent of my long-gone MG Magna and the figure urging on the steeds was brandishing a long whip. Imagine my surprise when I could discern the figure driving; it was Ben complete with black eye, yet not the Ben I knew; for he wore a gold collar and gold armlets. He gave his regal wave as of yore and beckoned me aboard.

We bowled along as in the old days and returned to the green land. There, the locals bowed as he passed between two obelisks, their surfaces carved with glyphs. The most prominent monument had a figure of Ben and I could only conclude that he was perhaps an Emperor, or a God, of these people as indeed he was; for I later found that he was Anulis, the God that guided dead souls through the Underworld.

I woke with a start. It was the early hours, almost dawn. I looked around and yes, there was Ben still lying there. Yet he was no longer there; for he had gone to his Valhalla of the Desert Sands.

Next day, with great sadness in my heart, I buried Ben in my backyard with no memorial or obelisk to mark the spot; only Malcolm, my garden gnome.

That night I wept.

THE READER OF MINDS

"It's the three wavy lines," I said.

"No! No! No! Concentrate Kenny. You still haven't mastered the code," and Jaikie shook his head in despair. "Try again!"

"I'm sure there must be an easier code than this convoluted one, Jaikie. Why don't I just use my fingers, one for circle and so on?"

Jaikie looked at me, thought and continued, "I think you just might have a point there. We'll try it."

So was born Kenny's ESP code.

Jaikie had arranged to take me along to the next meeting of the local Magic Circle and he thought it would be a good idea to use me as his stooge for the *World Premier* of his mind-reading act. After all, there was no way any of the other magicians would suspect that this 'innocent' layman was in on Jaikie's secrets. I was merely visiting as someone from the local press who wanted material for an article for his newspaper. Anyway, it would be good publicity for the Circle.

Come the evening of the visit and we arrived at the meeting's venue, the meeting of the local Magic Circle. I wonder why such clubs are always called 'Circle?' Perhaps it is the perception of a circle being an unending line, something that goes on forever, or that everyone on the periphery is equal, or just that everyone else calls their group a 'Circle.'

I entered the meeting place to find the group already gathered and about to begin. We were called to sit round the table (not a round table) as the business was about to start. The chairman banged his gavel and listed items on the agenda; this gave me a chance to look around the gathering. The first thing I noticed was that all were male, although I am assured that ladies are not excluded. Could it be that they (the ladies) have difficulty in keeping a secret! I'll ask later.

I was interested to find out why the various members had taken up prestidigitation (a posh word for conjuring). I looked around the assembly, at the various members, and noticed the glazed eyes of many. I could imagine that they were longing for the chairman to finish his spiel so that they could get on with the magic. Eventually he did finish to half-hidden sighs of relief and the different members pulled out their various tricks. As usual, these were chosen to be centred on a designated topic. So, on that particular occasion it was cards.

As I was that week's visitor, I was also the audience for all these tricks. And so I sat and watched endless card tricks which all seemed to do the same thing. Not only that, the tricks (they call them 'effects') must have been purchased recently, for frequently something went wrong. They had, no doubt, been practised once only – if at all. Then there was the complicated 'effect' which went on and on and on until I had lost completely the thread of the matter and my mind shut down. I now had that glazed look common in such situations.

Some members got into exclusive little knots and whispered secrets to one another while others nearby cocked their lugs to catch any little hints or whatever. Now for the big moment. It was Jaikie's turn to perform his mind-reading act. All gathered round with some interest, for they knew that he had considerable skill and he usually had something interesting to show. After all, he was one of the few 'pros' in the group.

Jaikie brought out his five ESP cards and spread them in a random line. With his back turned, he asked one of the members, Bob, to point to one card and think of that symbol while I took care to sit in Jaikie's line of sight. I duly gave the agreed sign. With his back still turned and to perk up the presentation, some questions and answers flew back and forth. "What is your birth sign? – are you left handed? – when did you arrive tonight? " and other irrelevant questions. "You chose the star sign." Much applause and puzzled frowns! I think he had hit on a winner there.

The meeting wandered on for some time with talk of magic and the latest advert on email, usually another card trick. All this made me wonder why these individuals took up conjuring in the first place. Often, it was a childhood interest which had re-emerged from the back of that dusty old drawer. For others, they had a feeling of power; they could do something that others couldn't. They are easy to identify, for when their trick is finished, they stand back and smile in a superior sort of way. Others, the professionals, do it for the money and they stick to a limited programme which suits their style, honing that programme to perfection. It is important that they entertain and thus the items must look like true magic to secure return gigs. This is the crux; the magic must entertain.

Things quietened as the meeting neared its close and Jaikie and I left them to coddle their secrets and whisper in corners.

Walking back to our cars, I could see that my companion was in deep thought. Opening his car door, he turned to me. "What are you doing tomorrow, Kenny?"

I just shrugged.

"Come round to my place about two. I have an idea and I'm looking for your opinion." Seeing my interest, he added, "Two it is, then." And with that he sped off.

I duly arrived *chez* Jaikie the following day and got down to business. He seemed all excited and soon I was to know the reason why.

"How do you fancy forming a double act along the lines of thought reading – mind transfer really," he proposed? "You know enough about the magic scene to make a sensible contribution and I'm sure we can put together an entertaining programme."

I hesitated at the idea. Although I had done some little conjuring shows, very minor things, in the past, I did not have Jaikie's vast experience. Certainly my knowledge of mind-reading was virtually non-existent. "Is there a market for a show? What sort of occasions would be suitable?" There were so many things I wanted to ask but his enthusiasm was contagious and I could feel myself catching the bug. His wife Meg made tea.

"Let's sit down and talk this through," he suggested.

Thus, that wet afternoon, we started scribbling plans. Wedding receptions are a good starting point but that would require a special type of programme involving walk-about magic which in turn meant a solo act. That is what he currently does and I could not see where I fitted in; but he insisted.

"I know, I know; but what I'll do is perform a programme around mind-reading and that will plant the idea," he suggested. "Then when a gig comes in for a party, say, we'll change to the double act that we are planning."

I could see the sense in that. Before leaving, however, there was the business of one key decision; what shall we call ourselves? "Two Minds as One?" No, I don't think so. It needs to be more personal, not some clever little phrase. "Jaikie and Friend?" Sounds too chummy! Perhaps something more mysterious and perhaps with a foreign name thrown in! How about, "Jacque le Blanc," and I'll just be your anonymous assistant – the one with the brains, I added.

That evening I felt quite elated at the idea of performing in this double act with the phoney name. I started to think of suitable tricks for a programme, things that didn't look like tricks.

Some days later we got together again to discuss more specific details and eventually cobbled together a show with enough variety to hold the interest of our audience. We then spent some weeks working together making minor changes here and there, ending up with a smooth show. We were all ready for our *Premier,* no! that should be *World Premier!*

Jaikie continued with the walk-around and table-hopping wedding gigs, at the same time spreading the idea of mind transferring entertainment. Then it happened. We got our first party engagement, a really posh hotel with a large function room complete with stage. This is when any snags would emerge.

At the hotel function, we presented our programme with

me as the assistant and Jaikie with his phoney French accent. The audience ood and aad and clapped at the right points. Matching the ESP cards in the Perspex frame was a big hit and in the 'post mortem' afterwards, we decided to put that last in future programmes.

The main outcome of that first gig was that the hotel decided to book us on a regular basis for future parties. Essentially we were kept busy over that 'wedding period' what with the concerts, adding to the act and polishing our technique. It was an enjoyable time.

There was one unfortunate incident which I now recall with different eyes in view of future events. After concerts, we always made a point of mingling with the guests. Inevitably there was the usual sprinkling of drunks, some of them quite harmless and a few awkward ones too. Jaikie with his vast experience handled these discretely and expertly. There was one occasion when, as it happened, many of the guests were known to us. One drunk accosted my friend with a great slap on the back and "Aw, Jaikie, I ken how ye dae a' these tricks. It's a' cheatin'."

"Oh yes, Rab! I expect some people cheat but not me." Jaikie was taking a bit of a risk there.

Rab was persistent. "All right, all right. What am I thinking, Jaikie boy?"

The incident was attracting some attention and I could see Rab's large wife hovering nearby. Jaikie stared in his most piercing, almost menacing manner. In his deep sepulchre voice he proclaimed, "You, Rab are thinking …" then slowly, almost from the grave, "You are thinking – I wonder when I should tell the wife about Jeannie Rankin?"

Rab's face turned white and his wife's face turned small, his eyes round and panic stricken, her eyes mere slits and mean. With considerable haste, they quickly merged into the tittering crowd.

Later after the party, Jaikie said nothing but I could see that he was unsettled by the whole affair. I decided not to pursue the matter and thought that he had picked up the information from one of the others.

We performed at a few more parties before the wedding season petered out. With a bit of time on our hands, we looked around for other outlets for our show. "We could perhaps mount a show at the Edinburgh Fringe," I suggested and for a bit we talked round the idea. Could we arrange publicity and a venue? It was a bit tight for time with only a few weeks to go; nevertheless we decided to give it a try.

We managed to arrange a venue, a former cinema. A bit large and expensive, perhaps, but we had little choice at this late stage and we decided to go ahead. Certainly the cinema was large and daunting with red plush all around, even red flock-papered walls, all a bit spooky; yet that was the sort of atmosphere that suited the act and we confirmed our booking.

It was a busy period: Tickets printed, posters printed and distributed, temporary staff engaged. We would need an electrician, a ticket collector for the door, some volunteers (free entry to the show for them) toting the tickets on Edinburgh's streets and a thousand and one other things as they came to mind. This was all new to us and there is no doubt that something would have been forgotten. Don't forget the risk assessment for the venue.

We both had a good look round the theatre and discussed how our act needed adaption. With this in mind, a thought came to mind. “Listen Jaikie, I have an idea. Do you fancy trying a blindfold act, you know, you sitting on stage with a blindfold, someone in the audience holds up an item and you name the item.”

He hummed and hawed a bit. “What about the method? We haven’t done this sort of thing before.”

I continued to develop the theme with growing enthusiasm. “It’s not all that different to what we do already. We start off with part of our existing programme; then I blindfold you and sit you centre-stage with a microphone and your back to the audience.”

“I’m with you so far.”

“Meanwhile, I dash up to the projectionist room, the one with the little window. I have an extension radio mike to your earplug and I’ll relay information about the item.”

“Unless it’s tiny. What if it’s tiny and you can’t see it.”

I persisted. “I’ll take my binoculars and use those.” I paused for his reaction. “Let’s give it a go. We can always go back to original plan. Oh, and here’s another idea.”

“You’re full of them today,” was Jaikie’s reaction.

“It’s to do with your appearance. Let’s make you more mysterious.”

Jaikie blinked and waited for elaboration.

I continued; “Slick down your hair, straight back and shave a little bit at the front to make a widow’s peak. It seems to be the fashion with mentalists.”

He went off grumbling and girning, yet I think he was

quite taken with the idea. It would certainly be in keeping with the act. And there he was shortly after with his new hairstyle seeking my nod of approval.

After a few days of hard rehearsal, the new act was all ready and we prepared ourselves for the opening.

We opened with a matinee performance and a total performance time of about an hour. As in other Fringe productions, entry was free and a collection would be made at the end as the audience left. A few visitors drifted in, I suspect out of curiosity and our programme duly started. There was mild applause at times until we reached the blindfold act. I could sense the enthusiastic reaction of the onlookers through the stronger ripple of applause from the albeit thin numbers. There was quite a rustle of paper money as the audience left.

As the week progressed, word got round and audiences grew. By the time we entered the second week the cinema was about three quarters full and we had to take on more personnel to handle the crowds and in particular to cope with the cash collection. By the Wednesday and with a large audience, my microphone developed a fault just as we entered the blindfold act. I shook the errant object and tapped it a few times, to no avail. It had gone dead on me. In a panic I looked up to see that Jaikie had continued with the performance. Not only was he naming the held objects, he was describing them in some detail. There was a lady's watch in detail complete with engraved inscription on the reverse side. Thus it ran on till the end with both me and the audience completely mystified.

Afterwards I met up with mystery man Jacque backstage, me baffled and Jaikie confused, completely washed out and drooped over an old basket chair. The chair squeaked and protested. He squeaked and protested even louder. "I really don't know what happened out there. I could hear you cursing and knocking your microphone, yet there was this sort of voice-over giving me all sorts of details – so I just went along with it."

We finished the gig (with a new mike) and packed up at the end of the week with something of a dark gloom hanging over everything. All the elation and enjoyment had gone and so we cancelled the third week and retired to our respective homes to have good ponder.

A few days later, I visited Jaikie at his home, drank his tea for want of anything stronger and sat on his best couch. Meg cleared off and left us to chat. For a time nothing happened and we just sat there looking at one another. Finally, I broke the silence; "What was all that about? What happened with the act? We had a good, entertaining show and just threw it away." I felt let down by his reneging.

Jaikie turned to me. "I know what you're thinking, Ken. I mean, I literally know what you're thinking. I really can read minds."

I stared at him in silence and shuffled uneasily. "You can read what I'm thinking?"

"Only when I concentrate on your mind. The thoughts don't just come flooding in at random. I have to concentrate on a specific mind and then it ... just happens."

My mind churned round with all sorts of thoughts; great stage acts; all sorts of mind acts. We could make our fortunes; I included myself in on any future deals, a bit presumptive really. There was no reason why he needed to include me.

Jaikie interrupted my thoughts (which he was probably monitoring anyway). “It bothers me greatly; it’s a great strain picking up people’s true views and opinions. When you think about it, if MI5 or 6 or whatever, found this out, they would recruit me as a spy. I could be used for all sorts of dubious schemes.”

I could see that he was deeply upset and thought it best to leave him to his own thoughts unsullied by mine, mercenary as they were. I bade Meg and Jaikie goodnight and left him to settle for a time.

That time was shorter than I expected, for a few days later Meg phoned urging me to call round to see her husband, indeed, to go as soon as I could. I duly arrived less than an hour later only to find Jaikie sitting very upright and staring into space, almost as though he were paralysed. I sat too, not knowing what to say; I’m not very good at handling such situations.

“He’s been like this since he came back,” Meg ventured. “See if you can find out what’s wrong, Kenny,” she pleaded. “I’ll go and make a cup of tea,” the panacea for all ills.

“Is there anything I can do, Jaikie?” I asked and managed to kindle a vague response. He blinked a couple of times and turned his attention to me and moaned something. At last there was the start of some sort recognition.

With a great sigh, almost of exasperation, he exclaimed; “I should never have started this mind reading caper.” He sat there, rocking back and forth. “It happened last week at old Joe’s funeral. I was just curious really. I wondered if I could communicate with the dead, so I concentrated on Joe in his coffin.” He moaned and swayed further.

I was ghoulishly curious to find out more; "And could you … ?"

"No! Not like that," he interrupted. "It wasn't like that at all. I couldn't get through in that way. It was his memory cells I linked with. The rest of the brain was definitely dead. It was like a memory stick for a computer. I could read all his memories, all his past, perceived wrongs, loves, hates, grudges, his whole history."

Jaikie was sobbing when I left. Meg was too. As I said, I'm not very good at handling such situations.

Sad to say, Jaikie is now in a sheltered home being looked after by Meg. This home is at the other end of the country so I seldom see him now. When I do, I see a shell overwhelmed by countless thought waves, a human conch shell with a sea of minds.

HIS KINGDOM

THE OLD MAN LOOKED AROUND at the familiar surroundings, a row of lime-washed cottages staring out at the ever-restless sea beyond the through road. Over there was an agéd jetty almost as old as himself. He well remembered helping to build it with tar washed timbers from some convenient wreck on Scars Rock. He was young then; he sighed and spat into the dust at his sea boots. His row-boat, with oars tucked under the seat, was tied to the jetty. It too spat into the occasional rogue wave.

The old man spent many winter hours caring for his craft. It was under cover in Dougie's shed to keep out the worst of the storms, although knowing Dougie, the shed itself could be doing with some care. Many an hour was spent scraping and sanding the boat's timbers down to the wood before applying the first thin coat of varnish. Further coats would follow and there ensuing, would be a rejuvenated vessel, his pride and joy. The boat had no name and was always just known as *The Old Man's Boat* for he seemed to have no name either.

On a mooring post, a lone gull perched. It too looked out to sea but with an evil eye as though planning the next mugging for vittles. On its cruel beak there seemed to be a smear of scarlet lipstick gone wrong, like the others of its species. On a whim it took off with an oath and a raucous rallying call to some distant rogue cousin.

The old man stirred himself from his dwam and set a course between red and green for The Creel o' Herring, the watering hole at the end of the village. It too belonged to Dougie. As he entered, the man himself greeted him. "You'll be having a drink then, Jimmy!" He called everyone 'Jimmy', hailing as he did from Glasgow.

The old man sat in his favourite corner with his glass for company. He rarely spoke, just sat there quaffing the ale, drinking in the banter. The air was full of sea-faring chatter, the talk of fish, of boats, of shoals and rocks; the time Hamish fell overboard and drank in half the Atlantic Ocean and then drank all Dougie's ale trying to rid the taste of salt. The air was full of smoke and tarry rope. That was his kind of place.

The crowd rarely spoke to the old man. They would look into his eyes and see the signs: *private, no trespassers.* He was part of the furniture and was accepted as such. He simply sat there in his corner, a hint of a smile and the occasional nod to an acquaintance; not to a friend for he had few of those still in the land of the living. Now and then, someone would whisper with others; they would talk about him, how old was he, his history, where he fished, for they guessed he was a fisherman; but in the main, he was just part of the furniture, old and gnarled and stained dark with time. And they would spit on the sawdust floor and talk of other things.

The old man up and left The Creel before the liquor-fuelled arguments started. It was dusk and the brighter stars had appeared as he boarded his craft and rowed into a gentle sea. He enjoyed this share of the day. He could lean on his oars and savour this tail end, the shy movement on the swell, the taste of salt and the hint of tar rope, the chuckle of wavelets on the stem. Here he could contemplate the meaning of life, of his life in particular and let the memories slip by. This was his domain, a realm of peace where he could let his mind wander through other worlds and think of the poetic experiences there. This was his Kingdom.

After a bit he dropped a line and pulled in a couple of mackerel and, as luck would have it, a whiting. "Mistress Thomson will enjoy that and I'll have the others for my supper," he thought. And the spell of the evening was broken as he returned to the staithe.

Later that year, the early autumn it was, and the wind was coming from the east. The old man took in the tether and pushed the boat away from the key as the dipping oar turned the prow into the chop; for with wind against tide, little combers had built up. It was one of those autumn evenings when the sky turned luminous and evenly bright, almost dazzling yet without any discernable cloud.

The boat drifted with the breeze and needed little guidance, only the occasional dip of a blade to keep it on course. The tidy craft jigged over the swell in the excitement of 6/8 time, enough to send a foot tapping; and the old man was pleased; with his back to the tide and sight of the village in the distance, he was pleased and leaned on the oars with a sigh. After a time, the featureless sky softened and dropped to kiss the water and the old man sailed into his Elysium Sea between the green starboard light and red.

Three days later, they found his boat some miles beyond the village bay. The remains of the old man were still slumped over the oars as they towed the craft back to the village. There they beached the boat and they buried the body in the kirkyard with due ceremony from the priest in mourning purple.

With a stone at his head, the old man faced the sea and his upturned boat on the shore. Scratched on the stone was simply, "Unknown Seaman." Soon, the stone and its legend merged with the moss and only the ribs of his boat jutted from the sand. Yet some say that they see him still in his corner in the Creel o' Herring with his glass of ale ...

He'd go into the cold air
And the wider silence and smile in it to see
The friendly water and himself waiting there.[6]

6 Norman MacCaig

MEN O' LEWIS

AWAY LONG AGO – OR even longer – there was an island, *Eilean Leodhais.* We know it as Lewis and Harris or simply Lewis; for Harris is graced by many mountains but seems a separate land. Nevertheless, Lewis has its own beauty with sweeping hills of heather, swathes of white sand and machair to the west, and rocky shores to the east. In those days, there was another beauty, a raven-haired priestess, Saeunn who held sway at the sacred place of *Callanish.*

Folk from round and about had differing opinions about Saeunn. Some thought she was a witch; some thought, a being from another world; others thought of her as a saint, for Christianity was emerging in this community. No matter! They were all agreed; Saeunn was different. On occasion, she would summon the locals to the *Callanish* stones to deliver an oration. Much of this they did not understand yet they enjoyed listening to the music of her voice. These sermons were delivered from the flank of the large central stone with Saeunn aye facing to the east, to the rising sun.

A favourite subject was her discourse on the battling factions of the island. These were forever taking the menfolk away from their work on their crofts. There would be no food for the dark times were it not for the women. They tilled the soil for crops, pulled wool from the sheep for clothing and cut peats for their fires. The audience agreed wholeheartedly, for it was mainly lassies from the populace.

"The men should stop their fighting and get back to putting their land in order," Saeunn exclaimed.

"You would be after telling us what we already know!" shouted old Biddy MacDonald who had had a lifetime of this. "While they are all away playing at Warriors and sodjers, we do a' the werk," she continued.

No doubt the Warriors and 'sodjers' heard about this and just dismissed it as idle chatter. They returned to their playing and their war games.

There were two main Warrior factions; there were the Macleods, sometimes known as the Black Tops mainly because of their black hair; and then there were the Norsemen showing Viking ancestry through blond and sometimes red hair. In effect, the skirmishes were half-hearted affairs with occasional cuts, skinned knees and a broken nose or even a broken arm. The winner was invariably the group with the most Warriors and the other group would melt away into the heather to fight another day and perhaps to win when they were numerous enough. The victors would cheer and sing of their victory; and that was that until the morrow. They would retire to the chief's Broch and celebrate drinking the night away with mead and with blaeberry ale. Inevitably with sore heads, bleary eyes and rough throats, they lost the next skirmish the following day.

So life continued for the Islanders of Lewis.

Now Saeunn was a bonny lass and was considered by many of the Warriors as a prize worth seeking. Her pale, almost white features were set off against the jet of her hair; her Norse blue eyes would turn to sloe when her blood was roused and the carmine mouth would set in a thin line. Any Warrior would think twice before approaching. In any case, she had set her heart on another; his name was Bjalfi.

The fair-haired Bjalfi was the court minstrel and would play and sing in the chief's Broch to the carousing rabble, part of their so-called victory celebrations. But there were occasions when he would wander to the machair with his clarsach and sing gently to the sea. There were times too when the selkies with their large dark eyes and sleek heads would join in with keening and Bjalfi would smile.

On one such day he sat among the machair flowers with his lap harp, playing a gentle air to the waves when Saeunn heard and was drawn to the strain. She sat beside him on the machair and hummed to the tune.

"What does your tune say, minstrel, in such a sad fashion?" she asked.

Bjalfi paused a moment and turned to the beauty. "It is a song of the sea as told by the Kelpies. They sing of its tenderness; how shy and demure it can be and yet in a flash it will turn to a maelstrom and destroy all before it." And at that, a great wave crested up the beach and bowed to the couple.

The minstrel sang another song, a song to the hills. He sang to the hills and they replied with conundrums and puzzles about their birth; for these were the oldest hills ever and their heather flanks cast echoes to the heavens. Still they lay there among the pink clover, with the ox-eyed daisies and harebells for company. Later hand in hand, they walked to the croft behind the Hills of *Bernara* as the sun set over Loch *Roag*.

All this did not go un-noticed and there were murmurings among the Warriors, the Macleods and the Norsemen and jealousy was afoot. Amid the outrage, some slunk away; and Bjalfi departed this life that night. He was cut down by a broadsword and his clarsach smashed on a Macleod's stane dyke. It lay there, its ribs exposed to the moon and its gut spread like some obscene stook of grasses.

Come the morning, Macleod of Macleod heard of this barbarous act. His minstrel had been slain by some mysterious unknown. Some blamed it on Finn the Squinter, but no-one believed them, for he was blamed for every mishap; and the Warriors and Norsemen wandered off to play more desultory war-games at *Camus Uig*. Macleod of Macleod fumed and the walls of the Broch rang with his calls for the blood of the perpetrator.

There was foreboding and much grief as Saeunn placed the body on a peat barrow and dragged it to the highest point of *Bernara*. There between a cleft in the highest rock, she placed Bjalfi and covered him with a cold gneiss tablet lined with white banded spar. The villagers mourned with her but dared not approach; for all they could see was a figure set as cold as the rocks around. Blood stained the white linen of her dress as she stared beyond *Loch Roag* to the horizon. "From here he can enjoy his beloved hills and the restless sea below."

In a dwam, Saeunn moved down the hillside to the standing stones of *Callanish*. She stood there beside the central stone for some time gazing to distant horizons as dusk gathered in a blood-red glow behind. The air chilled and clamped her body in its dewy grasp. So she stood all night and as morning dawned, she had decided. She would seek the help of the Gods of her ancestors.

Turning to the east, she called on Odin, the supreme God to help her avenge her cruel loss.

"Hear me, great Odin, great God of my ancestors," she cried again and again throughout that day, her voice echoing across the rolling hills of Lewis to the mountains of Harris. Morning turned to day and still she called.

As the reds of evening touched the west, great thunder clouds gathered and a crackling touched the sky. The clouds trundled and rumbled their way nearer and it seemed that the scrolls and whirls on the stones of *Callanish* glinted and throbbed in the fading light. A great peal of thunder broke the spell and seemed to be the signal for Saeunn to state her request. "Oh Great Odin, send me your son Vidoarr, Master of Vengeance to help me in my task. The dross that call themselves Warriors must go. Turn them to stone, I ask you Great Odin, that the seas may grind them to pebbles and further to sand, to be scattered along our shores." These words went echoing … echoing … till all of Lewis heard; even Macleod of Macleod; even the co-called Warriors gathered on the shores of *Uig* Bay.

For a moment, it seemed that Odin reflected; yet he went further. He turned the felons to bone so that their grinding would be forever. At that, a great tsunami rolled up *Camus Uig* and buried the bone figures – all except Finn, the Squinter, who lived to tell the tale.

Saeunn returned to her croft and lay on her cot for four days, exhausted by her efforts. After all, she was expecting a child.

In the days, the weeks, the months that followed, old Biddy MacDonald took Saeunn under her wing, feeding her porridge and brose and an occasional egg from her treasured hens. When her time came, Biddy delivered the child, as she had done for many others. It was a boy and as Saeunn gazed at the miracle she exclaimed, "He shall be a great leader, a great warrior. He shall take the surname of his sire – Gillibride – and I think we'll call him Somerled."

Somerled MacGillibride did indeed become a great warrior and leader of men. He ruled over many islands from *Lorne* to *Man* and was known as Somerled, Lord of the Isles.

Time moves on and the rock of Lewis continues its journey north for another billion years.

POSTSCRIPT

In the winter of 1831, a fierce westerly storm hit the Lewis and Harris Isles, not unusual for those parts. It carried away great swathes of the sand from its shores and exposed a cache of several bone figures, later found by a local crofter scavenging the shores for any storm treasures. These figures were thought by the academics to be chessmen. Yet we know better; for how do they explain the warriors biting their shields in fear or the terrified expressions in their eyes?

Also by the same author

Books under the name A.C.K. Smith:

Applied Physical Chemistry Problems: McGraw-Hill Publishing Co. Ltd 1968
Applied Physical Chemistry Problems: Japanese translation, Hirokawa Pub. Co. 1969
Applied Physical Chemistry: C. Heald, A.C.K.Smith, MacMillan Press Ltd., 1974
Applied Physical Chemistry: C. Heald, A.C.K.Smith, English Language Book Soc., 1982
Falkirk Tryst Orchestra: The First 15 Years, Appeal Media, 2017

Books under the name Kennedy Smith:

Rubik Cubik Magik: KANDA Publications, 1982
Kennedy's Dictionary for Magicians: Serialised in The Magician (magazine) 2006
A Cantraip of Tales: KANDA Publications 2020